NERD GIRLS

Also by Alan Lawrence Sitomer

The Hoopster

The Hoopster: A Teacher's Guide

Hip-Hop High School

Hip-Hop Poetry and the Classics

Homeboyz

The Secret Story of Sonia Rodriguez

nERD giRLS

THE RiSe OF THE DORKASAURUS

ALan LawRence SiToMeR

Disney · HYPERION BOOKS

NEW YORK

For Sienna and Tracey...
and the inner nerd that lives in us all.

acknowledgments

With gobs of appreciation to the best two
folks with whom a nerdwad could ever hope to
work, Wendy Lefkon and Al Zuckerman.

Printed in the United States of America

First Disney · Hyperion paperback edition, 2012
10 9 8 7 6 5 4 3 2 1

V475-2873-0-12145

Library of Congress Control Number for Hardcover Edition: 2010029588

ISBN 978-1-4231-5507-2

Visit www.disneyhyperionbooks.com

have a 3.73 grade point average and my body looks like a baked potato. My eyes are brown, my hair is brown, and sometimes when I snack on too many fig bars and run real fast in PE, I end up with brown streaks in my underpants, too.

I'm not just un-cool; I'm anti-cool. I mean, I even know how to properly use a semicolon in a sentence. What could be more pathetic than that?

I'll tell you what's more pathetic: the entire life of Allergy Alice Applebee, that's what. She's got *Guinness Book of World Record* "sensitivities," the kinds that make her have to travel with a list of **Things to Avoid**. If she touches a mango she breaks out in a rash. If she eats wheat, her vision blurs. And if she, heaven forbid, comes into contact with any sort of nut, dried seed, or botanical kernel, her throat swells, her esophagus contracts, and her glands begin to expand as if she had been stung by a swarm of bumblebees.

Today the ThreePees are going to sit next to Allergy Alice in the cafeteria and eat peanut-butter-and-banana sandwiches on whole wheat toast with mango marmalade for lunch. Some students think Allergy Alice might explode. Literally, they think she's going to internally combust like one of those overfilled water balloons that blasts apart when kept on a water faucet for too long. But instead of H_2O flying everywhere, spleens, gastric valves, and parts of her pancreas are going to splatter against the lunchroom walls. At least, that's what they're hoping for. Word buzzing around class is that this will be totally YouTubal, the kind of video that could go viral. The ThreePees think it might even break the one million hit mark.

Gawd, I hate the ThreePees. They rule the 8th grade.

And they know it.

The ThreePees is a name that stands for, well … the three P's: Pretty, Popular, and Perfect. They're the girls who have all the friends, all the glamor, all the clothes, and all the attention. They have everything. It's not fair, especially to a dorkasaurus like me.

To parents and teachers, the ThreePees come off like innocent little angels, shining examples of everything a young lady can be. But inside the cruel cage of middle school, when there aren't any grown-ups around, the ThreePees are mean, power hungry, and bossy. They think they're better than everyone else, and all my life they've made me feel like a loser/geek/doofus/turd.

Of course, I've helped them out a bit.

Like once, in fourth grade, I was so eager to answer a math-a-thon question that I smashed the silver bell too hard and it broke into a thousand pieces, sending a hunk of flying metal across the room that drilled Brace Face Stace in the center of her cranium.

Everyone laughed, even as Brace Face Stace was being wheeled away on an ambulance stretcher with a Harry Potter–type lightning bolt etched into her forehead. I think she was woozy with a concussion, too, because all Brace Face Stace kept mumbling about as the paramedics rolled her out of class was, "Corns and cheese. Corns and cheese."

Another time, when I made a homemade halogen light for the science fair, I left the ground wire exposed, and when the teacher, Mr. Upton, went to inspect my handiwork, he got shocked so bad by the electrical current that his contact lenses caused a burn ring to form around his pupils. Now he looks like a man who is always staring at students with googly eyes, like he's from outer space or something.

Mr. Upton used to just be weird. I made him spooky.

But the worst was my birthday party in fifth grade, when I realized that if I pinched my nose and closed my mouth, I could blow a soft stream of air out of my right ear. So, thinking it'd be cool to blow out the candle on my birthday cake with ear air instead of mouth air, I turned my head sideways and prepared to dazzle my classmates with my supernatural, extraterrestrial, spectaculabulously amazing, one-of-a-kind abilities. However, being that I couldn't produce a very strong stream of ear air to blow out the flame, I had to lean in really close to the candle.

That's when I set my hair on fire. My classmates started screaming. I just thought they were excited about my supernatural, extraterrestrial, spectaculabulously amazing, one-of-a-kind abilities. Our teacher, Mr. Hanson, thinking quickly, ran over and began slam-dunking my head into the birthday cake. I had no idea what was going on as he smashed my noggin up and down and around and around into the frosting. He must have dunked me at least twenty times, rotating my ears so that the front of my face, the back of my brain, my cheeks, and even my eyebrows were free from any further flare-ups.

I almost drowned in cake icing.

Of course, the smoke from my burning hair ended up causing the fire alarm to go off. Oh, the joy of walking single file out to the soccer field with cake mush covering my entire skull. Per district policy, the entire campus had to wait thirty minutes until the fire trucks came and gave us the all clear to return to class. I wasn't even given a paper towel.

"Hey, what are you doing?" I said, pulling away from this weird sensation I felt tingling in my ear.

"I like frosting," Tommy Tardo answered. He pulled a finger full of white stuff out of my earlobe and plunked it into his mouth.

"*Ew!* Gross," I said.

Tommy Tardo licked my vanilla-flavored earwax and grinned. He had crooked teeth and a wandering eye. "Burned hair smells like toasted marshmallows. I like campfires. More, please."

"Excuse me?" I said.

"More, please?" he repeated with an outstretched finger. "Vanilla is the color of white dogs."

We haven't seen Tommy Tardo at school in a while. Rumor is, he was transferred to a school with soft walls.

It's like that with a lot of kids around here. From the outside,

Grover Park, California, might seem like a normal place with normal people and normal families, but once you're on the inside, forget it. This community is filled with wackos. It's like there was a crazy magnet put into the center of the earth, and all it does is pull the cuckoo birds here. From kids to parents to teachers, most everyone is nuts.

But nuts in their own "special" ways. *Sheesh!*

Back in class, I looked up at the clock on the wall. It was three minutes to lunch. Three minutes to eleven thirty. Three minutes until Allergy Alice's doom.

One of the ThreePees, Kiki Masters, spoke.

By the way, what kind of a name is Kiki? It sounds like some sort of Hawaiian fruit drink or something. Why the ThreePees always have the most exotic of everything when my name is Maureen—how boring is that?—is just another way that my life is totally and completely not fair.

Kiki (giggling): This might cause the biggest allergic reaction ever documented.

Brittany-"Brattany" Johnston (inspecting her pedicure): Urrgh, is my polish chipped?

Sophia "Sofes" O'Reilly (giggling back): Yeah, like more allergic than when that guy tried to jump his motorcycle over all those cars and totally crashed.

Kiki (paused and puzzled): A guy crashing a motorcycle isn't the same as an allergic reaction, Sofes.

Sofes (now puzzled herself): Oh ... yeah.

Brittany-Brattany (still inspecting her pedicure): Urrgh.

Kiki rolled her eyes, Brittany-Brattany picked at her toes, and Sofia O'Reilly flipped her hair and went right on being Sofes, a girl who would lose an intellectual battle of wits with a bottle of glue.

But goodness, did she have a nice nose. Just perfect. Sofes had the kind of nose that people put on Christmas cards. If there were justice in the world, one day a stray volleyball would fly through the air in gym class and smash her into pudding.

Okay, maybe that's mean. But the ThreePees are mean. Mean as snakes. Besides, I hate volleyball. That's because once in sixth grade they made us play and I went running to save a point, tripped over my shoe, hit a pole, and ended up getting tangled in the net like some kind of bluefin tuna.

Like I said, total dorkasaurus.

I looked up. Two minutes to the bell. Two minutes to lunchtime. Two minutes to the end of Allergy Alice Applebee as we knew her.

Unless . . . I thought to myself.

ook, I'm no hero. Don't know why I ever thought I should act like one either. I mean, new students at new schools who come in without knowing anybody at the start of a school year always get picked on by their new classmates, right? That's like a law of the universe or something.

At least it was at our school.

Anyway, the lunch bell rang, and little Miss Allergy Alice had the nerve to walk on over to a faraway table, off in the corner, away from the rest of humanity, all by herself, to start eating her de-skinned celery stalks or whatever nontoxic foodstuff she was allowed to munch on.

Yeesh, the gall of that girl. Every other kid in our class knew that Allergy Alice was about to be made famous on the Internet as the star of *The World's Biggest Allergic Reaction Ever Caught on Tape*, and there she was sitting all alone in the corner of the outdoor cafeteria like one of those stupid ducks waiting to get blasted by a hunter dressed in an orange safety vest.

Swim away, little duck, swim away! I wanted to scream. But ducks are obviously not the most intelligent of creatures, because if they were, they'd have long ago figured out a way to outsmart overweight, middle-aged goobers-with-guns who spend their Saturday mornings standing in the tall grass blowing quack-quack sounds.

Not that I have anything against hunting innocent little cute fuzzy feathered animals with submachine guns or anything.

The ThreePees made their move. They looked like some sort of middle-school S.W.A.T. team. Kiki, flashing hand signals, crossed the courtyard and sat down next to Allergy Alice on her left. Sofes O'Reilly followed and zipped to her right. Brittany-Brattany Johnston smoothly slid in and took a seat directly across the table from the weirdo girl.

And out came the sandwiches.

Allergy Alice, surrounded, must have thought at first that some of the kids at her new school were about to make friends with her. But then, when Brittany-Brattany reached into her purse and took out a cell phone video camera, the new girl musta realized that she was being set up. After all, she was boxed in.

Like a duck.

Each ThreePee began to unwrap the cellophane of her sandwich. The stage was set.

So let the show begin, I thought to myself. Let the show begin.

I stormed over.

Before any of the ThreePees knew what hit them, I snatched

up the peanut-butter-banana-and-mango-marmalade sand-wiches right off the table.

"A-ha!" I screamed. TheThreePees were stunned. Shocked. Entirely caught off guard. It was a masterful sneak attack.

My plan, it had worked!!

But I didn't really have much of a plan beyond grabbing the sandwiches, so after ripping the weapons of torment from the hands of these evildoers, I decided to really make my point by . . .

By eating their sandwiches in front of them.

Not just eating them, but really stuffing them in there. Defiantly. I wanted to prove that this was the end. No more! Forever beyond this moment the ThreePees would no longer rule our campus. People weren't going to take it anymore. People were going to stand up and fight. People like me would have to be dealt with. The rule of tyranny was over!

I stuffed one, then two peanut-butter-banana-and-mango-marmalade-on-whole-wheat-toast sandwiches into my mouth and gave a deep, menacing squint of my eye. No more! I thought, No more, you jerkfaces!

I crammed them in really good.

No more!

The ThreePees sat stone silent. They were totally in awe. I'd never experienced such triumph.

Then, being that there was no more room in my mouth, I began to squish the other sandwiches in my hand. Really crush them, like Godzilla would crush a car in one of those monster movies. And I continued to stare, too—to glare at the ThreePees with a dark menace in my eye.

Then I spoke.

"Take that!" I screamed.

But actually, it sounded more like, *"Mrmph mrmph!"*

Okay, so the peanut butter in my mouth made it hard to talk, but still, I was feeling good. Feeling strong. Feeling empowered.

"Mrmph mrmph!" I yelled again. "This is for the little guy. This is for the underdog. This is for the people who get bullied by meanie-snobs like the three of you!"

I squished with extra force.

"Well, not in my house, bay-bee. Not in my house today!"

It all played out beautifully. Except it sounded like this:

"Mrmph mrmph!! Mrmph mrmph rumff bloomf! Mrmph mrmph klemtthh blrrrp phlim sconf!"

Then I began to jump up and down and yell at the top of my lungs, screaming as if I had just won a gold medal at the Olympics.

"Mrmph rumff bloomf klmmtthh!" I shouted. *"Mrmph rumff mrmph bloomf klmmtthh!"*

Bread crumbs flew out of my mouth. Bits of mango sailed like missile shots from between my lips. But I didn't care. It was over. It was finally over. The ThreePees would never rule this land again! I'd never basked in such sandwich-squishing glory.

Then I looked up. Brittany-Brattany was videotaping me.

Videotaping me?

Yep, videotaping me. Videotaping the whole thing. The face stuffing. The mouth spitting chunks of jelly and bread. The jumping up and down like a monkey at the zoo while babbling incoherent phrases such as *"Mrmph mrmph mrmph!"* She'd recorded it all.

Oh no! I thought.

I did the only thing I could think of.

I RAN!

My eyes bugged out and I dashed off. Of course, the Three-Pees chased me, Brittany-Brattany taping me the whole time.

I ran toward the bathroom. But Kiki was faster and blocked my path to the door.

I ran toward the water fountain. But Sofes was faster and prevented me from getting a drink.

I ran toward the classrooms. I ran toward the nurse's office. I ran toward the fire exit door, the kind with the warning sign on it that says "DO NOT OPEN THIS DOOR OR ALARM WILL SOUND."

No matter where I ran, they cut me off. I was boxed in.

Like a duck.

"What in the world is going on here?" shouted Mr. Piddles as he came charging up to investigate the chaos. Every student in the cafeteria area was watching.

Kiki spoke first.

"Maureen stole our lunches."

Mr. Piddles stared at me with a disapproving teacher's glare, the kind that indicated I was about to be in really big trouble. He waited for an answer.

"*Mrmph mrmph rumff bloomf,*" I said.

"And she used a lot of bad language, too," added Kiki.

"*Mrmph rumff blrrrp phloonth,*" I replied in my own defense.

"And then she threatened to sock me. To punch me in the nose."

Mr. Piddles glared at me, the top of his bald head turning red.

He was one of those antiviolence teachers who had been picked on his whole life for loser-ness, so the threat of one kid bopping another was an especially touchy subject with him.

"Yeah," added Brittany-Brattany, "we were just trying to make friends with the new girl, make her feel, you know, welcome, and Maureen freaked out."

"*Mrmph mrmph rumff bloomf,*" I protested. "*Mrmph mrmph rumff bloomf.*"

"Like, uh, yeah," added Sofes. "We were just trying to make the allergy weirdo feel tolerated, and this blimped-out wacko went all bonkers on us. Like, uh, where's the sensitivity for others this school always preaches?"

Sofes rolled her eyes as if she had just made a really good intellectual point. I rolled my eyes too. Mr. Piddles wasn't actually going to believe them, was he?

Of course he was.

Mr. Piddles glared at me, his egg-shaped head starting to glow like a hot red coal in a furnace.

"Did you steal their sandwiches?" Mr. Piddles asked, crossing his arms.

I gave a last-ditch effort at trying to gulp down the peanut butter and unstick my stuck-together mouth, but the back of my throat was glued to my tongue as if I had swallowed a container of wet cement or something. It was hopeless.

That's when I realized it was over. Silenced by peanut butter, handcuffed by palms covered in mango marmalade, sweating like a pig from trying to outrun three faster girls around the courtyard, they had me. Once again, the ThreePees had me.

I lowered my head.

"I am only going to ask you this one more time," Mr. Piddles repeated. "Did you steal their sandwiches?"

"*Nrmph,*" I meekly responded.

Mr. Piddles took me by the arm.

"Justice must rule, Miss Saunders," he said as he began to escort me away. "For without justice, society is lost. Come with me."

"But don't be too hard on her, Mr. P.," said Kiki in my defense as I was being led away. "She's kinda got self-esteem issues, you know. About her weight."

Kiki turned to me with pretend kindness in her eyes.

"Aw, don't feel low, Maureen," she said in a gentle voice. "You're just..." She took a moment to think of something really delicious. "Big boned. That's all."

Kiki looked at Brittany-Brattany and gave a little nod.

"Yeah, Maureen, you're just big boned," Brittany-Brattany responded.

"Yeah," added Sofes, also pretending to be concerned about my feelings. "You're not some kind of fat-butt, plump-o blob with an eating disorder. You're just big boned."

Even Mr. Piddles rolled his eyes at that one. But, angry as he was, all he cared about at that moment was justice. My justice. As a social studies teacher, he was obsessed with it.

"Let's go, Miss Saunders," instructed Mr. Piddles, escorting me out of the courtyard and into detention. "You must now pay your debt to society."

And that's when it happened, the worst of it all. As I was guided across the lunch area and taken away to what I knew was sure to be a horrible doom, past the ThreePees, past the cafeteria workers, past all the students in my grade, my worst possible nightmare came true.

I saw Logan Meyers. Yep, Logan Meyers, the Greek god of middle-school boys was staring right at me.

And laughing his butt off.

I dropped my head. The ThreePees had won again. Won big-time.

Intellectually, it made no sense for me to have a crush on Logan Meyers. He was so far out of my league that I may as well have been playing one-on-one basketball against Kobe Bryant. But this crush didn't come from my brains. This was a DNA crush. It came from genetics. Biological composition. The flames of the heart. Logan Meyers was like jelly doughnuts to me: I knew I shouldn't even look at them, but in the chromosomal content passed down to me by my ancestry, my genes screamed "I NEED ME SOME SUGAR-SUGAR!!!"

And who can fight their DNA, right? When it came to things like cupcakes, French fries, and Logan Meyers-es, I don't even know why I tried to resist. It was pointless, like heredity or Darwinism or something.

Logan Meyers is actually the reason I had taken up the clarinet. According to my band teacher, Mrs. Marks, playing music could make your problems disappear.

Of course, when I played the clarinet, cats screeched, but that was their problem. My problem was to figure out how to stop liking a boy who would never in a million years ever stoop to the level of liking me. Not so easy even if I was willing to learn every instrument in the jazz band.

When I finally got home that afternoon, after writing on Mr. Piddles's chalkboard I WILL NOT STEAL THE LUNCHES OF MY PEERS 500 times (could there be a stupider punishment than writing standards on the board until my hand felt like it was going to fall off?), I picked up my clarinet, aligned my fingers just like Mrs. Marks had taught me, thought about my pathetic dorkasaurusness in life, and blew a high C.

Out came a long stream of bubbles.

"What the..." I thought. Then it hit me. I tasted soap.

I spit and spit and spit. *Bl-uck*.

"*MART-EEEEEE!!*" I shouted.

I ran downstairs and flew into the kitchen.

"What's the matter, Boo?" asked my mom. Ever since I was a little girl, my mother called me Boo. She meant it in an affectionate way, but it always made me feel like when she found out she was pregnant with me, the news scared her so much, it was like *Boo... you're gonna have a baked potato*.

"Marty filled my clarinet with liquid detergent, and now my mouth tastes like the floor of a Laundromat!" I said.

"Wasn't me," answered Marty, without looking up from the table, where he was tinkering with some kind of electronic gizmo.

"Marty..." asked my mother, "did you fill Boo's clarinet with dish soap?"

"Wasn't me," he repeated. But of course we knew it was

Marty. He was the king of the practical joke. From covering the toilet seat with Saran Wrap when I was being potty trained so that the pee-pee leaked all over my leg, to turning my alarm clock forward a few hours every now and then so that some mornings I was up and ready for school by three thirty a.m., to putting spicy vapor rub in my training bra so that my nipples felt like they were going to burn off when I first started preparing for "womanhood," my brother, Marty, was Mr. Bag-of-Funny-Tricks.

Yeah, real funny.

"Ma-homm…" I whined.

"Maar-teee…" said my mother with a mildly disapproving look.

"Sorr-eee," Marty answered, confessing to the crime. And that was the end of that. In my mom's eyes, severe discipline had been just been handed out, and she was quite confident that Marty, never wanting to face such wrath again, would never, ever dare to prank me in the future. After all, who could stand up to such fearsome punishment?

I stared at Marty's secret black bag. No matter where he went, he had this black bag with him, and inside was every type of practical-joke tool ever invented on the planet. I lunged for it, but I was too slow, and he pulled it away.

"You stink at the clarinet anyway," said my sister, Ashley, as she walked into the kitchen while sending out a text message on her phone. "Like you stink at everything."

"Shut up, Ash, before I pound your face into meatballs," I answered.

"Now, that's not nice, Ashley," interjected my mom. "Maureen is very talented."

"At what?" asked my younger sister, smacking some bubble gum and still not looking up from her phone.

"Yeah, at what?" I asked.

"Well..." said my mom, taking off an oven mitt and starting to think. "Let's see. You are special."

"Vague," I answered.

"Unique."

"Also vague," I added. She paused. I waited. This was going to be good. All my life my mother kept insisting to me that I was talented. That I had gifts. That I had something to offer the world that no one else could offer.

"You have to remember, Boo, you're like a snowflake," she said with cheery encouragement. "You're entirely distinctive in this world."

"Yeah," said my punk sister. "You're distinctively on YouTube."

"Huh?" I said.

"Maureen is on YouTube! Maureen is on YouTube!" Ashley darted off into the other room to fire up the computer. The rest of us followed.

A minute later we were staring at YouTube, at a newly posted video called A Chunky Chick Does the Peanut-Butter-and-Mango-Marmalade Big Butt Dance.

It had been up less than an hour and it already had 847 hits.

I watched in horror as it started to play. Ashley giggled and began texting her friend.

YEP I C IT!

Marty the butthead laughed. My mother looked at me like I

was a sad, pathetic puppy dog who wasn't even going to be given the dignity of being drowned in a lake.

Me, I headed for the stairs, went to my room, and closed the bedroom door behind me. The only sound I heard was the hysterical laughter of my older brother and younger sister as I shouted *"Mrmph mrmph rumff bloomf!"* and squished peanut-butter-banana-and-mango-marmalade-on-whole-wheat-toast sandwiches like some sort of demented dancing fat girl freak from outer space.

The ThreePees weren't just mean...they were cruel.

y mom let me stay home sick from school the next two days. She told the office that I had a bit of a temperature. I told her I was suicidal.

"You shouldn't joke about things like that, Boo," she said. "You're a very special, very talented person, and one day this is all going to seem like small potatoes."

"Mom," I said, looking her straight in the eyes. "The Chunky Chick Does the Peanut-Butter-and-Mango-Marmalade Big Butt Dance is never going to seem like small potatoes. Never, ever, ever."

"Just wait, Boo, you'll see," she answered. "'Sometimes in life, if you want to have rainbows, you gotta have rain.'"

I rolled my eyes. This is exactly why my dad had divorced her. While everyone else saw reality, my mom saw bright, cheery, positive stuff—all the time. And what could be more annoying than someone who always saw the bright side of things when you were crazy depressed?

"Come on, Mom," I said, heading to the cupboard, "give it a break."

"You watch," she replied.

Six cookies should do it, I thought. For a start.

"How 'bout an apple, Boo?" she suggested as she saw me fill up my hands with deliciousness.

"Mom, this situation calls for chocolate," I answered. "It's what I like to call a *double fudger*."

Mom watched as I plopped some dark brown love into my face hole. The world might have been cruel and rude and mean and hurtful, but chocolate understood me.

Chocolate loved me.

"Oh, Boo . . ." said my mom in an uplifting, supportive tone. "No need to catastrophize."

Catastrophize? Where did she come up with these words?

"Sometimes," she added, "what seems like the worst actually brings about the best. You just never know."

I rolled my eyes and plunked another cookie into my mouth.

"You just never know," she repeated, to make her point.

And then, to make *my* point, I repeated my cookie plunking. Twice more.

Despite all of this repetition, my mom still would not let me repeat my "please call the school, and tell them I am sick" routine. I argued, but she wouldn't budge on a third day home.

"But I have scientific proof I am suffering from the Indonesian mumps," I said.

Silence.

"Combined with vertigo."

Still nothing. I upped the odds.

"Complicated by symptoms of Africanized bacterial meningitis," I argued. "I swear. I found it on the Internet."

Mom gently patted me on the shoulder, told me I'd be fine, and not to trust everything I saw on the World Wide Web.

I sulked my way back to my room.

The entire night was spent biting my fingernails and freaking out about my return to school the next day. Well, not just my fingernails. I bit some chocolate-covered graham crackers too. A person's gotta do what they gotta do to make it through the night, right?

The next day, when the car stopped to drop me off, I felt tears forming in my eyes. I didn't want to get out of the minivan. Like, I really, really didn't want to get out of the minivan. And how sad is that when you don't want to get out of a minvan?

"Gimme two minutes before you come out, Maureen. I don't want anyone to see me with you."

"Ash-leee," warned my mother in another one of her disapproving tones. Oh yeah, I'm sure after that kind of scolding, my sister would never dare ridicule me again.

"Just kidding, Mom," said Ashley with a fake smile as she slid open the door. Then she held up two fingers and mouthed the words "Two minutes." After all, she had a social life to think about.

I guess I couldn't blame her.

I remained where I was, stuck to the seat. Mom being mom,

she smiled warmly, and then told me that when you fall off the horse, you gotta get back on.

Really, those were her exact words.

"When you fall off the horse, you gotta get back on."

"But the horse broke my butt," I answered. "And no one sits in a saddle with a broken butt."

"Well, now your butt matches your face," said Ashley, reaching back into the car. "Sorry, Mom, forgot my lunch."

Mom, once again disapprovingly rolled her eyes. Really, I'm not sure how Ashley handled such ferocious motherly fury.

"Two minutes," Ashley mouthed again, and then she disappeared.

My mom looked at me with a cheerful, encouraging smile. However, as soft as she was on the outside, I knew there was no way in the world she was going to let me stay home from school another day. It wasn't fair. With me, Mom was always the toughest.

I slumped out of the car, didn't say good-bye, and moped toward class. And if I'd thought I was a loser/loner/nerd/geek/dorkasaurus before I'd done the Chunky Chick Does the Peanut-Butter-and-Mango-Marmalade Big Butt Dance, now I felt like one of those contagious kids that could give the whole school head lice.

And no one wants head lice. Not even your best friend.

My two best friends were, of course, nothing but a distant memory these days anyway. They had both moved away last summer because their dads worked for the same company, and they had both lost their jobs in the bad economy. Go figure.

Cyndy went to Texas, Rachel went to Idaho, and though the Web allowed the three of us to keep in touch, it just wasn't the same through texting and stuff and all. And now there wasn't a respectable person on my campus that was ever going to talk to me again.

At least not without laughing in my face.

I hung my head as I shuffled sadly through the halls. Earth was nothing more than a cold, bitter rock floating aimlessly in outer space.

A cold, bitter rock with homework. How depressing is that?

I was alone on a lonely planet. Until lunch, that is.

Of course I sat at a table all by myself. Of course I never expected anyone to approach me unless they planned on making fun of me. And of course I packed cupcakes. Three of them. The world may have hated me, but baked goods were the last of my loyal comrades, and despite the fact that my mother had put asparagus spears and a no-skin chicken breast into my lunch bag, I was able to sneak in my own private triple play: chocolate, vanilla, and Mr. Lemon.

No, there weren't many good things about Grover Park Middle School, but at least it had Paradise Palace right across the street. Paradise Palace was a convenience store that specialized in the cheapest kind of junk food sold on the planet. They had honey buns filled with brown ooze, doughnuts dunked in green sludge, and pieces of pink cake that looked so artificial they must have been baked in an oven in a nuclear waste dump.

Truly, there wasn't a piece of real fruit anywhere in the store. Not even an overripe banana. Just junk food. Adults might have hated it, but for a kid like me, the place across the street was truly paradise.

Hey, maybe that's where they got their name, Paradise Palace?

"*Ahhh*," I said staring at the day's only joy.

Sitting all by myself, I chomped into life's last remaining bliss. Mrs. Marks was wrong about the clarinet. Music couldn't take your problems away—but cupcakes stuffed with synthetic yellow cream could.

Mmmm. The lemon drenched my tongue. Then, as I went in for heavenly bite number two, out of the corner of my eye I saw Beanpole Barbara approaching my table.

Beanpole Barbara?

At first she didn't say anything. Not a word. All she did was sit down at the far end of my table and try to act casual.

I stared at her. She avoided eye contact with me and tried to look relaxed and innocent.

Then, a moment later, she slid over. Just an inch. I continued to stare. Beanpole Barbara looked up at the sky as if she were watching the clouds roll by or something, just another regular ol' day in a regular ol' world with regular ol' birds flying through the air. I waited, wondering, What in the world is Beanpole Barbara, the klutz of the century, doing right now?"

She moved a little closer.

Then a little closer.

All the while, Beanpole Barbara looked at the clouds. Soon enough she had slid all the way down to the end of the bench so that she was sitting right across from me. However, since she was pretending to be watching the clouds instead of watching where she was going, Beanpole Barbara took another slide and then fell right off the end of the seat, and she crashed to the ground with a gigantic *thud!*

"Ouch," she said, rolling in dirt.

"What on earth are you doing?" I asked.

Beanpole Barbara didn't answer. Instead, she nodded her head and waved to someone who was hiding behind a tree.

"C'mon," Beanpole Barbara whispered, with another nod. "C'mon."

Suddenly, Allergy Alice appeared from behind a thick tree trunk. After shuffling her feet for a moment, she walked over. Barbara got up from the ground, and they both sat down across from me.

"Oh, don't tell me," I said, rolling my eyes.

"G'head" said Beanpole Barbara, trying to get Allergy Alice to speak. "G'head."

Allergy Alice paused, then opened her mouth. But she didn't speak. Instead she raised an inhaler the size of a scuba tank to her lips and took such a big wheeze off of the thing it sounded like she was the daughter of Darth Vader.

Wheeesh-whooosh. Wheeesh-whooosh.

I stared at her like she was a freak.

"G'head," said Beanpole Barbara one more time.

Allergy Alice raised her eyes and looked at me. "Why'd you stand up for me?" she asked.

There was a pause. They both stared and waited. I shook my head.

"'Cause I'm stupid, that's why," I said. And that was the truth. I mean, why a plumpy person like me would choose to stand up for a walking immunization clinic like Alice by eating a picnic basket's worth of peanut butter sandwiches in front of the entire school remains a mystery to me.

"'Cause I'm stupid," I said again.

"Well, I didn't think it was stupid," said Beanpole Barbara. "I..." Beanpole paused. "Thought it was brave."

"Yeah, well, you're not the 1,043rd hit on YouTube either, now, are you?" I replied.

"5,468."

"Huh?"

"5,468," Allergy Alice repeated. "It's getting kinda popular."

"Great. Thanks for the update."

"Accurate statistics, they're important to me."

"What?"

She didn't answer. Instead she just nodded her head and raised her scuba tank again.

Wheeesh-whooosh. Wheeesh-whooosh.

The three of us sat there for a moment in silence. Suddenly, Beanpole Barbara tried to throw something perky into the conversation.

"You know, you're not stupid, you're..." she blurted out, trying very hard to be uplifting. "You're big boned."

I glared.

"Please, never say that again."

"Okay," she answered, then she smiled with extra perkiness as if we were really getting somewhere.

I shook my head. More silence followed. The awkward kind.

A bird chirped.

"We should be friends," Beanpole Barbara suddenly declared.

"Excuse me?" I answered.

"You know, friends. The three of use should be friends."

I looked over at Allergy Alice. She took another slurp.

Wheeesh-whooosh. Wheeesh-whooosh.

The stupid bird chirped again.

"We can't be friends," I answered. "The best we can be is associates. Look around. We're like the leftover grapes in the bottom of the bowl. Nobody wants us."

I scanned the groups of kids in the lunch area, chatting together, eating together, laughing together. All the real friends, the people who had chosen to be with one another because they wanted to, not because there was no one else to spend their time with.

"Naw," I repeated. "The best we could ever be is associated grapes."

"Sometimes I like to smell my belly button lint."

"What?" I said, fairly horrified.

"Sometimes I like to smell my..."

"I heard you the first time, Beanpole," I snapped. "But why would you say such a thing?"

"Because friends," she answered, "they share secrets."

"I hate secrets," I said. "And I am terrible at keeping them."

There was another awkward pause.

"And to think," I added with a groan, "these are supposed to be the good years in my life."

"You're funny," said Allergy Alice, looking at me with a goofy grin.

I raised my eyes and stared, waiting for another *wheeesh-whooosh*, but it didn't come.

Then it did.

Wheeesh-whooosh. Wheeesh-whooosh.

I knew it. I just knew it.

"Well, look who it is, the Three Little Doofuses," said a voice from behind me. I felt a surge of terror crawl up my spine. I had known it would only be a matter of time before the ThreePees showed up to make us low people feel even lower.

"Beanpole Barbara, Big-Boned Maureen, and Allergy Alice Applebee," said Kiki Masters as she wiggled over and took a seat. Of course her two pet donkeys were with her, Brittany-Brattany Johnston and Sofes O'Reilly. "So, what's the four-one-one, nerd-o-las?"

"Yeah, like, been on YouTube lately, Maureen?" asked Brittany-Brattany with a smirk.

I stared at the ground.

"Leave her alone, Kiki," said Beanpole Barbara with some fight in her voice. "Maybe she likes being on the Internet, huh? Maybe she likes being famous, huh? Maybe she likes that the entire world saw her do her fat little *Mrmphh Mrmphh* dance with sandwiches? Ever think of that? Huh? Did ya? Did ya?"

I raised my eyes. *Was that supposed to be some kind of defense of me?*

"Oh, right," said Sofes O'Reilly. "Just like when that kangaroo totally took a bath in the river."

Kiki and Brittany slowly turned to Sofes and crinkled their foreheads.

"Excuse me?"

Sofes tried to backtrack. "Maybe it was on the History Channel," she added, as if that made any sense at all.

Just then, the bell to end lunch rang. And thank goodness, too. Time to go back to class. I gathered up my stuff and rose from the table.

"Have a good afternoon, loser," said Kiki, with bite in her voice.

"You too, Kiki. See you after math."

"Not you, Sofes!" snapped Kiki. "I was talking to Big-Boned Maureen and her dork squad."

"Oh..." answered Sofes. "Yeah. Have a good afternoon, dork squadders."

The ThreePees stood, grabbed their fancy backpacks, and began to wiggle away. But before they were gone, Sofes turned around and fired another dart in our direction.

"And we mean it!" she shot.

"Uh, mean what, Sofes?" asked Brittany-Brattany.

"Um...you know...that," answered Sofes, looking back at the three of us. Hand lotion probably had a higher IQ than Sofes O'Reilly.

Then they were gone.

Beanpole Barbara stood and immediately began to mock the ThreePees by trying to wiggle like them when she walked.

"Have a good afternoon, dork squadders," she said in a high-pitched voice. However—*Bam!*—she crashed into a tree.

"Ouch!"

Beanpole Barbara, not having seen the stationary tree, which had probably been in the same spot for, oh, about a hundred years or so, then walked back over with a large red welt on her forehead. "Don't worry, I'm okay. I'm okay."

"Who's worried?" I said. Her bump began to swell.

"Really. I'm okay," she said, then *Bang!* Beanpole bent down to reach for her backpack and smashed her head into the table.

"Ouch!" she yelped again. "Don't worry, I'm okay. I'm okay."

She raised her head. Now there were two red bumps. Her wounds made her look like some kind of baby goat that was starting to grow horns.

Suddenly, Allergy Alice spoke. Actually, it was more of a mumble.

"What's that?" I asked, turning around. "I didn't hear you."

Allergy Alice stared into the distance like some kind of Wild West gunfighter.

"Girls like them, you gotta hit 'em where it hurts."

Then, still staring into the distance with a dangerous squint in her eye, Allergy Alice raised her scuba tank.

Wheeesh-whooosh. Wheeesh-whooosh.

"Hit 'em where it hurts 'em bad."

Who were these freak-a-zoids?

5

"We're in!"

That's how Beanpole Barbara approached me the next day. Declaring, "We're in!"

Then she ran up to the lunch table and smashed her knee into the bench so hard it sounded like she cracked a bone.

"Ouch!" she yelped.

Her collision caused my grape juice to spill. But thinking quickly, Beanpole Barbara made an effort to catch the container before it fell over entirely.

That's when she smashed her elbow.

"Ouch!!" she yelped again.

That second crash sounded like she'd need a sling.

"Don't worry, don't worry, I'm okay, I'm okay," she said, holding her arm like a wounded bird.

"Who's worried?" I said, as I stared at my spilled drink. But there went my daily dose of nutrients. I mean, that thing contained three percent real fruit juice.

Oh well. I tried.

Ignoring her injuries, Beanpole Barbara sat down across from me, away from the purple puddle on the bench.

"Did I mention we're in?"

"Did I mention I was gonna drink that?"

"Sorry."

A moment later, as if this was some kind of prearranged meeting, Allergy Alice walked up and sat down next to Beanpole.

Right in a lake of grape juice.

"So, we're in?" Allergy Alice asked.

I sat there waiting for her to realize that she had parked herself in a puddle, but she didn't say a word.

"Yep, we're in," answered Beanpole.

"In what?" I asked, though I knew I probably shouldn't have. And why hadn't Allergy Alice flinched or something from the juice pond she had plopped into?

"In the talent show!" Beanpole Barbara exclaimed. "Haven't you seen the flyers around campus? Every year the ThreePees win the thing and get their picture in the yearbook, and every year they rub it in. So I say, let's beat them at their own game and get OUR picture in the yearbook for a change."

"Like I said yesterday," added Allergy Alice, flashing another Wild West gunfighter squint, "hit 'em where it hurts."

Then, sure enough, out came the scuba tank.

Wheeesh-whooosh. Wheeesh-whooosh.

"What's in that thing?" I asked.

"Inhibitors," she answered.

"Inhibitors?" I said. "What kind of inhibitors?"

Allergy Alice paused, raised her eyes, and stared at me with a serious look.

"I think I peed my pants."

"You're sitting in juice," I informed her.

"Oh," she replied. "I thought I felt something."

There was another pause.

"Aren't you going to get up?" I asked.

"What's the point?" she replied. "It's pretty much all soaked in by now."

"It's grape," I said. "Gonna stain."

She sat there for a moment thinking about it. "I've dealt with worse," she answered.

I stared.

"You're strange," I said.

"You're funny," she responded.

"I'm not trying to be funny," I told her.

"I'm not trying to be strange," she replied.

Then out came the scuba tank.

Wheeesh-whooosh. Wheeesh-whooosh.

Had aliens landed and no one sent me an e-mail?

"So," said Beanpole, interrupting our highly thoughtful conversation, "are we gonna do this, or what?"

"I'm in," said Allergy Alice.

"I'm in," said Beanpole Barbara.

They both looked at me with hope and excitement.

"Naw," I told them. "Not me. I'm out."

The table got quiet. I could feel their disappointment. We began to eat our lunches. Allergy Alice had some cut fruit, some cut vegetables, and a gluten-free, wheat-free, taste-free, organic granola bar. Beanpole Barbara had an egg salad sandwich with the crust trimmed off. Actually, it had more than that trimmed off. Her lunch had been shaped into some sort of dazzling eight-point starfish.

I stared at Beanpole's food. I'd never seen such a fancy sandwich.

"Is this gonna bother you?" Beanpole said to Allergy Alice, pointing to her lunch before she took a bite.

"Eggs don't bother me," she answered.

"Good," said Beanpole Barbara.

"But chicken feathers make the bottom of my feet itch," Allergy Alice added.

"I'll write that down," I said, fascinated by this piece of information. Then out came Mr. Lemon.

It was back-to-back cupcake lunches for me, but that's only because it would have gone stale if I didn't eat it by that afternoon. You know how cupcakes are. Some places only sell them four to a pack, and if you don't eat them all by day three, the frosting dries out.

I prepared to take my first bite.

"But why not?" Beanpole asked, wanting an answer from me.

"'Cause what kind of talent do you have anyway?" I shot back, setting down Mr. Lemon.

"Um, I dunno," she answered. "Let me think for a sec."

"And what about you, Q?"

"Q?" repeated Allergy Alice with a shrug, not understanding the term.

"Q, that's what I'm calling you," I replied. "It's too long to call someone Allergy Alice every time you want to speak to them, so your name is Q, which is short for Question Mark, and your name is Beanpole."

"Why Question Mark?" Q asked.

"Because every time I look at you," I answered, "my brain is filled with questions."

"Oh good, we're nicknaming. That's what friends do," said Beanpole, with perkiness. "Isn't that right, Moo-Moo?"

Slowly, I turned.

"Mo-Mo?" she offered.

I glared.

"Just plain Mo?" she suggested.

"If you must," I replied. "If you must."

I think the blaze in my eye scared her.

"Gotcha," she answered.

"So, like I said"—I turned back to the allergy oddball—"do you have any talent, Q? Any talent at all?"

"Wait!" exclaimed Beanpole before Q could answer. "I have a talent. I can swab my ears with a Q-tip."

"So . . . who can't?" I replied.

"Yes, but can you do it using your toes?" Suddenly Beanpole started to unlace her shoes.

"Stop, stop," I said, checking around to see if anyone was looking at us. "Even if you can clean you ears with your toes, that's not a talent, that's circus freak stuff."

Beanpole dropped her head, dejected.

"Let's face it," I continued. "Between the weirdo girl being allergic to air, you bonking into every cement object that exists on this planet, and me being the star of a ridiculously embarrassing YouTube video that already has eight thousand hits…"

"Twelve thousand six hundred and eighty-three."

I stared.

"It's 12,683 hits as of 7:19 this morning." Q shrugged. "I told you, accurate statistics are important to me."

"Well, thank you for the latest numbers," I replied with a ton of sarcasm in my voice. "But you forgot to take a slurp off of your deep-sea diving tank to add the extraterrestrial sound effects for me."

She stared like a lost kitten.

"You're funny."

"Stop saying that!" I said. "We're losers. Don't you get it? We're all losers."

Q and Beanpole looked at me with wide eyes.

"We are the duds in life," I continued. "The doofs. And any time we try to play with the big dogs we're going to be embarrassed, okay? So if you'd kindly just let me eat my cupcake lunch in peace, I would greatly, greatly appreciate it!"

Ouch, I thought as soon as the words left my mouth. That was harsh. But then again, they needed to hear it. And better for them to hear it from me now before they learned it the hard way by being humiliated onstage in front of a whole universe of people in some talent show that was rigged for the ThreePees to win anyway. I mean, didn't they know that not only had Kiki won it every year in middle school, but her older sister JoJo had

37

won it every year in middle school, and that their oldest sister, CeCe, had won it every year in middle school before them? The Masters sisters had owned the Grover Park Middle School Talent Show for something like eight years in a row.

Even their mother had won it back in like the 1900s or something, when she went to Grover Park Middle School. There was just no way possible for us to win. I wasn't being mean; I was simply saving Beanpole and Q from the hurt, shame, and embarrassment, even if they were too stupid to realize it.

"Um...Mo..." said Beanpole.

"I don't want to hear it," I answered.

"But, Mo..." she said, trying to get my attention.

"No, Beanpole!" I replied, and though Beanpole and Q might not have understood things at the time, one thing was for sure...Mr. Lemon did. I raised him up to my nose, took a deep inhalation of yellow-flavored love, and prepared to take my first bite of lunch.

"Hey, fat girl, try a carrot!"

SMASH!

Just then, someone pushed my hand up into my face, forcing me to ram the lemon cupcake up my nose.

From chin to eyebrows, I was covered in gooey cream.

"Ha-ha!" said Kiki.

"Smile, big bones!"

Snap!

Brittany-Brattany took a photo.

"Har-har," screamed Sofes. "That's the way the cupcake crumbles!"

Kiki and Brattany paused, amazed by Sofes sudden cleverness. They each gave her a big high five.

"Good one, Sofes!"

"Yeah, well," she replied, "you can't always judge a cover by its book."

The three of them giggled away, another fun victory in the life of being a ThreePee.

It took a moment for me to realize what had actually happened. Slowly, I scraped the lemon frosting from my eyes. Then, through a creamy haze, I saw a horrible sight.

Logan Meyers. Laughing at me.

Laughing his butt off.

Wow, I must have been good for chuckle after chuckle, huh?

A moment later, I turned around and saw Q and Beanpole. They were staring at me. Just staring. Scared and hurt and nervous and afraid and frightful.

That's when I stood up. But I didn't just stand up; I straightened my spine, puffed out my chest, and calmly began to pack up my things.

"Practice will begin after school at my house at four fifteen," I said in a firm, even voice. "And, ladies, don't be late."

With that, I walked away...to go clean the frosting out of my schnozz.

"Y ou registered us as what?" I said.

"The Dorkasaurus Mafia."

"I thought you said the Doofasaurus Mafia," replied Q.

"No," answered Beanpole with a shake of her head. "The Dorkasaurus Mafia is much more intimidating than the Doofasaurus Mafia. It's the hard *K* sound in *Dork* that gives the name some fire."

"Hey," I said. "I have an idea. Maybe we should call ourselves The Dipstick Mafia? That'll really scare 'em."

Q and Beanpole looked at one another, seriously considering my suggestion.

"Nah."

"No."

"Nuh-unh," they replied. "People might make fun of us."

I rolled my eyes as I approached my front door. Really, I couldn't believe I was going through with this. Who would have ever thought I'd be a part of a Dorkasaurus—or Doofasaurus —or Dipstick—or whatever-it's-called Mafia, trying to win the world's stupidest talent show? But this wasn't about friendship; this was about business.

The business of revenge.

"Okay, look, there're a few rules," I stated before we entered my house. "So listen up."

Q and Beanpole raised their eyes and gave me their full attention.

Well, aside from a short break for scuba.

Wheeesh-whooosh. Wheeesh-whooosh.

"Inhibitors?" I said, waiting patiently.

"Exactly," Q answered.

"Can I begin now?" I asked when it appeared she had finished her latest deep-sea dive.

"The stage is yours," she answered.

"Thank you," I said with a sigh. Oh, this was gonna test me.

"Okay," I said. "Couple of things you need to know before we go in. It's like the zoo in there. Don't feed the animals."

"You have animals?" asked Q with a fearful look. "Pet dander makes my nostrils close."

"Not real animals! Family animals. Brothers and sisters and mothers and things." I could tell they didn't fully understand. "Just don't interact with anyone, okay?"

"But why?" asked Beanpole. "At my house my mother always makes pumpkin bread shaped into the first initials of my guest's last names and serves them with ginger tea when I have people come over."

"And when was the last time you had people who actually wanted to come over, Beanpole?" I asked.

"First grade," she answered.

"Exactly," I said. "Look, just trust me on this."

I opened the door. The two girls behind me bonded.

"You know, pumpkin rind causes my arm hair to fall out."

"Right or left arm?"

"Both. On Halloween, I have to wear a wet suit just to go trick-or-treat."

"Wow," replied Beanpole. "Do you get a lot of candy?"

"I shouldn't really eat candy," answered Q. "I'm the kind of kid who likes it when people give out pencils."

"I like pencils too. Hey, Maureen," asked Beanpole, "do you like it when the houses give out pencils for Halloween?"

I stood there for a moment as the question hung in the air.

"Do I look like the kind of girl that likes it when people give me pencils when I trick-or-treat?"

They didn't answer. We entered.

"Aw, Boo, you brought some friends over," my mom said, with a smile that was a mile wide when she saw the three of us come inside. Oh no, here we go, I thought. "You should have told me you were bringing friends," Mom said.

"They're not my friends, Mom," I answered. "They're peers. From school. We're . . ." I had to think of something, but something that wasn't the truth. "We're working on a project together. Gotta get started. Time is short."

"Well," said my mom in her never-be-defeated-by-a-negative-thought type of way, "maybe your 'peers' would like some cookies?"

"Don't bother, Mom. This one," I replied, pointing at the Beanpole, "doesn't eat things that aren't geometrically designed by a licensed architect, and that one only drinks stuff like non-wet water."

My mom looked confused. No time to explain. I had to get them into my room before Marty or Ashley showed their ugly faces.

"Okay, peers . . . upstairs."

I pointed upward. Q and Beanpole started to walk.

"I'll send something up anyway," said my mom in a cheery tone. "You never know."

"Don't bother, Mom."

"Don't be silly, Boo."

Whatever, I thought.

"Wow, look at all these trophies," said Beanpole as we climbed to the top of the stairs. "Which ones are yours?"

I shot her an evil look. My brother, Marty, was some kind of inventor who won science fairs and stuff like that. My sister, Ashley, was a gymnast. A really good one. For some reason, God had decided to give all of my athletic ability to Ashley and all of my creative ability to Marty. Not a trophy in our house had been won by me.

Actually, there was one. Once at summer camp I had tied for third place in an archery contest. They didn't give me an actual trophy though, just a ribbon. But Mom put it on the Saunders Hall of Fame mantel anyway.

Oh the envy that must have been felt by every parent who had ever visited our home. I, middle child Maureen, was the third-best eleven-year-old archer out of seventeen kids at Camp No-One-Gives-a-Poop.

Really, who could compete with that?

I threw open the door to my room.

"Out!" I said.

"I'm allowed to use the computer too! It's for both of us."

"Out! Or I'll smash your face like a walnut."

"I'm telling Mom," whined Ashley.

"G'head," I snapped back. "And write your congressman too. Now out!"

Ashley shot me a look of sisterly hatred and then started making her way to the door.

"Hi," said Beanpole Barbara in a perky voice as they met by the door. "I see you're a junior Olympian gymnast. That music they play must really inspire you."

"What music?" snipped Ashley.

"You know, the Olympic music." Then she started to hum the Olympic theme song. "Dummm—dummm da-dummm-da dummm dumm. Dumm dummm dumm dumm-da dumm-da dumm dumm."

All of it. She was humming the whole darn concerto.

"Dumm dummm dumm dumm-da dumm-da dumm dumm. da-dummm-da dummm dumm. Dumm dummm dumm dumm-da dumm-da dumm dumm."

Ashley wrinkled her forehead and glanced at Allergy Alice with a look of disbelief, as if she were saying, "Can you believe this dork?"

Q smiled, then lifted her scuba tank.

Wheeesh-whooosh. Wheeesh-whooosh.

Ashley bolted for the stairs.

"Ma-homm," she screamed, as she ran for the kitchen. "Maureen brought freaks into the house."

I looked at my two peers.

"Didn't I tell you not to interact with anybody?" I said. "Didn't I?"

They each looked at me, confused. I closed the bedroom door.

"Never mind. Let's just lay it all out on the table. What kind of talents do you have?"

We sat on the floor and made a little circle.

"Well, I can swab my ears with a Q-tip."

It took all the strength I had not to reach over and strangle her. "We already covered that, Beanpole!"

"Oh...yeah," she said. Then, after a moment she added, "Well, I think we should reconsider."

"Reconsider?" I said. "Why would we reconsider? I mean, this is exactly why the two of you don't have any..."

I stopped.

"Okay...I'm listening," I said, trying to be patient. "Why I'm listening, I don't know. But I am. G'head. Why should we reconsider?"

Suddenly, Beanpole sprang to life.

"Well, what if...what if...wait...What if I didn't swab my ears with a Q-tip. What if I swabbed YOUR ears with a Q-tip?"

"Using your toe?" I asked for clarification.

"Of course, using my toe. I mean, how stupid would that be for me to swab your ears with a Q-tip if I were just using my hands?"

"So, let me get this straight," I said, on the verge of blowing a blood vessel. "Are you saying it would not be stupid to have an audience full of people watch you clean out my earwax with your toe?"

"I'm saying it would show talent."

I turned to Allergy Alice. "Do you have anything at all to contribute to this conversation?"

She paused. "You're"—*Wheeesh-whooosh. Wheeesh-whooosh. Wheeesh-whooosh*—"funny."

"I'm gonna kill myself. Really, I should just end the pain now." I stood up. "Tell me, Q," I said in a fit of desperation, "does slurping off of that thing give you any kind of superpowers?"

"Superpowers?"

"Yeah, like can it help you to leap over tall buildings or fly through the air, or, I don't know, help clean eye boogers from your friend's pupils?"

"Earwax," said Beanpole, for clarification. "I clean earwax. I am not sure I'd trust my toes working around your eyes."

"So making me deaf is fine," I said, "but making me blind presents a problem for you?"

"What?"

"I said, so making me deaf is fine, but making me blind presents a problem for you."

"What?"

"I said . . ."

"What, I can't hear you," said Beanpole. "I'm deaf. Get it. I'm deaf? Ha-ha!"

I wasn't going to last much longer. "Okay, I'm going downstairs to look through the garage. Maybe we can build something. Stay here. I'll be back in a minute."

I jumped up, exited the room, and closed the door behind me. *Deep breaths, Maureen. Deep breaths.* That's what I told myself as I headed downstairs. We'd been at this less than five minutes and already I was prepared to kill both of them.

"Twenty-two grand," said Ashley in an annoying, stick-it-to-me way as I passed through the living room.

"Huh?"

"You just hit the twenty-two thousand page-view mark on YouTube," she added. "And just so you know, sometimes they move you up into the bar at the top of the main welcome page once your video clip starts to get a lot of interest."

"Great," I told her.

"Just thought you'd want to know."

"You're the best, sis," I said, and headed into the garage.

Junk. That's all there was in our garage. Junk. The Three-Pees, I am sure, were probably choreographing some kind of cheerleader extravaganza featuring flipping and flying and fireworks, and here I was looking through garage junk trying to figure out how to compete with them.

That's when I saw the black bags. At least, that's what they were known as in our house. My dad, when he bailed on us, had left a pile of stuff, and though us kids had wanted to throw it all away many times over, Mom told us to keep it because one day they might prove useful.

Or we might want them.

Or we might learn something valuable about our father from them. Or about ourselves.

Buncha positive mumbo jumbo. At this point in my life, my dad didn't mean squat to me. Never even thought about him, or the way he'd just run out on the whole entire family without any warning. But we did keep all the stuff, though I don't think any of us had ever opened it since the day he'd flown the coop.

And I certainly wasn't about to open it just then, so I grabbed a broken vacuum cleaner, a few old packs of Play-doh, and a box of tacky Christmas ornaments.

Maybe one of the bozos upstairs could juggle? I returned to my room.

I entered and saw Beanpole and Q sitting on my bed, flipping through one of my sister's stupid teenybopper magazines—the kind I never read.

I grabbed the magazine from under their noses and tossed it onto the floor.

"Why'd you do that?" asked Q.

"'Cause we have work to do," I snapped. But the real truth was, I hated the way those magazines always made me feel— like I was never thin enough or never hot enough or . . . well, just never enough. Stupid magazines just showed me all the things I would never have or be.

Beanpole sat up, crossed her legs, and started bouncing up and down like a bobble-head doll.

"Do you need to pee or something?" I asked.

"No," she replied. "It's just that I'm having so much fun."

"I'm so glad," I answered.

"Is it okay if we dive in now?" she asked. "We waited for you, Mo."

"Dive in to what?" I replied.

She pointed. I looked over and saw a plate of cookies.

"Where'd those come from?" I asked.

"Your mom sent them up." Beanpole reached for one. They

were Oreos, America's favorite. "I think we should have a toast," Beanpole said.

"A toast?" I said.

"Good idea," replied Allergy Alice as she reached for a cookie.

"Wait," I said. "Can you even have an Oreo? I mean they're not gonna, like, cause your tongue to evaporate or anything, are they?"

She rolled her eyes. "Can I have an Oreo? Geesh, I'm a kid, ain't I? I mean, my doctor probably wouldn't want me to, but hey, you only live once, right?"

She grabbed a cookie and raised it high. Then Beanpole took her cookie and raised it high as well. They waited for me.

I looked at the plate of Oreos. Like I was gonna pass up on those. I grabbed a cookie.

"A toast," said Beanpole. "To taking down the ThreePees!"

"And to getting our picture in the yearbook," added Q.

"And to not entirely humiliating ourselves," I added.

"And to"—Beanpole paused as she thought of something really perky to add—"the Nerd Girls!"

"The Nerd Girls?" I repeated.

"Hey, I like that," said Q. "To the Nerd Girls."

I shrugged my shoulders. I guess it couldda been worse.

We clanked cookies and had our first official toast, each of us popping an entire Oreo into our mouth at the same time in one big, delicious bite.

A moment later we all went "*Blah!*"

"*YUCK!*"

"*EW-WW!*"

We started spitting and scraping the cookie from our tongues.

"What's in those?" asked Allergy Alice.

"That's the worst cookie I ever tasted," said Beanpole.

"Where did you"—*spit-spit*—"get these?" I asked.

"From your mom," said Beanpole. "Your brother brought them up."

"My brother?" I said. *MAR-TEE!* I screamed.

"Why, what's"—*spit-spit*—"wrong?" asked Beanpole.

"What's wrong is that my brother"—*spit-spit*—"scraped the cookie cream"—*spit-spit*—"out of the middle of these Oreos and replaced it"—*spit-spit*—"with toothpaste."

"Toothpaste?" said Beanpole. "Why would he"—*spit-spit*—"do that?"

"'Cause he"—*spit-spit*—"thinks it's funny."

"Toothpaste?" said Q. "But I'm allergic to mint!"

"Allergic?" I asked. "What"—*spit-spit*—"happens?"

Before she could answer, I started to see what would happen. Mint made Q's ears turn red. Really red. Like fire-engine red.

"Can I have a washcloth, please?" she asked politely. "With ice?"

Her ears began to puff up like one of those cheapie inflatable plastic rafts you buy for a swimming pool.

"Uh, yeah . . . sure," I said, and went downstairs.

Q's throbbing lobster ears caused our talent meeting to end early. Not that we were really on the road to getting anything accomplished, but still, there were better ways to call it a day without turning someone into Dumbo the Flying Red-Eared Elephant.

"More ice?" I asked as Q held washcloths to the sides of her head.

"Naw, I'm good," she answered. We stood out front and waited for her mom to pick her up. It took Mrs. Applebee no time at all to get to my house.

Allergy Alice's mother zipped up to the curb and threw her car into PARK.

"I'm sorry about the toothpaste," I said as Q began walking toward the vehicle. Her mother jumped from the car, looking panicked.

"It's okay," answered Q. "My ears will probably go back to normal by Thursday."

"Are you okay? Are you okay?" asked Q's mom, taking a look at her daughter's ears. "Do you want to see Dr. Fishman?"

"I'm all right, Mom," Q said.

"Let's go see Dr. Fishman. Gotta be safe. Gotta be safe." And with that, without even introducing herself to us, Allergy Alice's mother put her into the car, and they zoomed off.

Boy, she was really concerned about the toothpaste. Had something more serious happened than I thought? I looked at Beanpole.

"Maybe this is, ya know, a bad idea," I said.

"What are you talking about?" Beanpole answered as she put on a pink bicycle helmet. "When you were downstairs, Alice told me she was having the best time she'd had in years, despite her scalp being on fire."

"Her scalp too?" I said.

"Mint's really hard on her system," Beanpole said. "But this is like, so much fun! For me too. We're having the best time."

She fastened her chinstrap and climbed aboard her bike.

"Remember, we're the Nerd Girls. Nothing can stop us." She

began to peddle away, raising her right hand high in glorious triumph. "Nothing!" she shouted.

And then she crashed into a parked car.

"Ouch!"

She bounced up with a chunk of pink helmet missing.

"Don't worry, don't worry. I'm okay," she said as she hopped back onto her bike. "See you tomorrow, Mo!"

I turned and went inside, too scared to watch Beanpole operate something as dangerous as a bicycle. That girl didn't need a safety helmet; she needed body armor.

I walked into the kitchen.

"She's allergic to mint, butthead."

"Wasn't me," said Marty with a mischievous smile as he tinkered with yet another electronic gizmo. I eyed his black bag.

"What happened, Boo?"

"Nothing, Mom," I said. "Other than Marty and Dad just showed how they are perfectly related."

"Your father?" said my mom in shock. It'd been years since any of us had seen him or even mentioned his name.

"Yep," I said. "Just like Dad, right, Marty? Not caring who you hurt or how you do it just as long as you have a good time yourself. Stupid jerk."

I headed to my room.

"What's she talking about, Marty? Your father?"

"Nothing, Mom," Marty said in low voice. "Nothing."

hough the sun was shining and the weather was warm
and pleasant, Q showed up to school the next day wearing earmuffs.

The fluffy kind, with spots like they were made from Dalmatian fur.

"Hey, doofus girl, moving to Alaska?" Kiki said with a huge
laugh as the ThreePees cruised over to our lunch table.

"Or Hawaii?" said Sofes, trying to really rub it in.

I swear that girl would need fifty free bonus points to score
fifty-one on an IQ test.

Kiki sat down next to me. "I understand you ladies joined
the talent contest," she said.

"Remember, Keek, they're calling it an Aptitude Demonstration this year," said Brittany-Brattany, taking a seat as well.
"They want to be all politically correct."

"Whatever," replied Kiki. "The point is, you dud-o-las don't actually think you have a chance of winning, do you?"

"Yeah, do you?" asked Sofes.

Kiki reached for a piece of my bubble gum. I had brought four packs to school to eat after my apple. Trying to cut down on the caloric intake and all.

She put a piece of my gum in her mouth and then blew a bubble to taunt me.

"I mean, you must realize that you have no chance," she added.

"Oh yeah?" I said, and then I blew a bubble of my own right back at her.

"Yeah," she replied, and then she blew another bubble, this time slightly bigger, back at me.

I reached over, took another piece of bubble gum out of the pack, and put it in my mouth so I could add a little more bulk to my bubble.

I chewed and chewed, getting past that first wave of sugar.

"Oh yeah?" I said, and then I blew a big bubble, the kind that was definitely intended to send a message.

Beanpole smiled. Brattany and Sofes stared at Kiki, waiting for her to make the next move.

Kiki, not to be outdone, reached for two more pieces of gum. She chewed to get it soft.

"Oh, you think so, do you?" said Kiki, and she blew a mammoth bubble.

Aw, heck no, I said to myself. This wench doesn't want to get into a bubble blowin' contest with me.

That's when I opened the second pack and plunked three pieces of fresh gum into my mouth.

It took me a minute to chew and chew and chew to get it all soft. There was so much sugar in my throat, I had to gulp it down twice.

Allergy Alice looked up as I was chewing. Our eyes met. I could see she really wanted me, needed me, to nail this victory. And the fact that she was wearing those silly Dalmatian earmuffs was kinda my fault anyway. I mean, if it hadn't been for my stupid brother, well...I owed her this one and I wasn't gonna let her down.

I began to blow.

And blow and blow and blow. It was the biggest bubble I'd ever created. It was bigger than the first one I had blown, bigger than Kiki's bubble, bigger than my whole, entire head.

It was the biggest bubble ever blown on the campus of Grover Park Middle School, I was sure of it.

Take that! I thought.

Pop! Kiki reached out and stuck her finger into my bubble. Gum exploded all over my face. It went past my chin, around my ears, and into my hair.

Kiki and her pet donkies stood up as I sat there with a face covered in pink goo.

"Remember," said Kiki, "we always win."

Brattany took out her camera and snapped a photo of me —*click!* Sofes gave a little airhead giggle. A moment later, they walked away.

"Son-of-a-no-good-mother-frazzler-nufkin..."

"You had her, Maureen. Nice job! You had her!" Beanpole exclaimed.

"Excuse me?" I said. "In case you're not aware, my cranium is covered in chewing gum."

"No, she's right," said Q. "You had her. And for a minute, she was scared. Did you see the look on Brattany's face? She was nervous. Them witches"—*Wheeesh-whooosh. Wheeesh-whooosh*—"we got 'em on the run."

On the run? I thought. I might have to shave my head.

"Ooh, we're gonna get 'em."

"And it's about time."

I'd never seen Beanpole and Q so excited. I stood up.

"Hey, where're you goin'?" asked Beanpole.

"Oh, nowhere," I replied. "I mean, I guess I should just sit here WITH A HEAD COVERED IN SUGARY GOOP FOR THE REST OF MY LIFE!"

I screamed. They stared. For a moment it was silent.

Finally, Q spoke.

"You're"—*Wheeesh-whooosh. Wheeesh-whooosh*—"funny," she said as she readjusted her earmuffs.

I shook my head and stood to walk away. Then I stopped. Of course, who else?

Logan Meyers. All smiles at the pink-faced bubble gum girl with chewing gunk in her ear holes.

At least my relationship with Logan wasn't one of those up-'n'-down rocky ones. I mean, we were steady as a cuckoo clock. I would show up at school, the ThreePees would embarrass me, and the silent, secret supercrush of my life would get a huge laugh-his-butt-off chuckle every day during lunch.

That's the key to strong relationships, you know. Consistency.

Our next big meeting was at Beanpole Barbara's house. Or, as I like to think of it, the Department Store.

Why the Department Store? Because every time I go into one of those really nice department stores, into the Homes section, everything is just perfect. From the way every pillow is fluffed to the way every sheet matches every bed comforter to the way all the towels in all the bathroom displays have been color coordinated to match the wallpaper and the floor coverings.

That was Beanpole's house. It was like the nicest department store I'd ever visited. Matter of fact, I was nervous to walk across the white carpet because it looked as if it had been vacuumed in a way that created a symmetrical floor pattern, like virgin snow or something.

"Oh, you must be Maureen," said Beanpole's mom, stepping out of the kitchen to greet us when we entered. She was wearing a checkered red-and-white apron that made her look as if she wasn't really a resident of the house; she was more like a floor-model mom who simply worked at the Department Store. "And you must be Alice," she said. "May I take your earmuffs?"

"No thank you," said Alice.

"Very well," replied Department Store Mom. "Cookies are baking, and tea will be served soon. Please, make yourselves at home and let me know if you need anything."

And with that, Department Store Mom walked back into the kitchen.

She hadn't even messed up the virgin white carpet where she'd walked. Weird.

"Oh hey, sporto," said Beanpole's father when we walked into the living room. He was wearing a plaid colored sweater vest over a white collared shirt and tan trousers.

"Let me come give you a peck," he said as he put down his magazine, rose from his chair, and walked over to kiss his little girl on the cheek.

"We do that every day when she comes home from school," he said to Q and me with a glowing smile. His teeth were so white he could have been in a dentist commercial.

Yep, Department Store Dad.

"I'm Alice," said Q, extending her hand for a shake. I did the same thing.

"I'm Maureen," I said. We shook. His hands were soft, like he had never picked up anything in his entire life more rough than a bag of silk.

"Well, I'll let you gals get to work. I know you've got some big stuff in the making. While I was carving the roast beef last night, you two were all my little princess here could talk about."

Beanpole blushed. I wondered if they had carpet stain remover in the kitchen for when I puked on their floor. This perfect family stuff from the 1950s was straight out of a television show.

Department Store Dad disappeared to go buff his leather slippers or something, and Beanpole took us to her room. As we walked through the halls, I saw all their family pictures on the walls.

Beanpole as a little bean. Department Store Mom in her department store wedding dress on their department store wedding day. And Department Store Dad.

Wearing sweaters.

I looked more closely at the pictures. I'd never seen so many sweaters worn by one man. He had photos in zip-up sweaters, pullover sweaters, V-neck sweaters, turtleneck sweaters, and crewneck sweaters. Wool, cashmere, cotton, Department Store Dad had them all.

I nudged Q to look at all the photos and spoke quietly so Beanpole couldn't hear me. "I bet if this guy goes swimming, he wears a sweater in the pool."

Q looked at me and squinched up her face.

Wheeesh-whooosh. Wheeesh-whooosh. "I don't get it."

"Aw, nothing," I said, moving on. "Let's just get to work."

A moment later we walked into Department Store Daughter's bedroom, otherwise know as the Pillow Department. I'd never seen so many pillows on a bed before. Pink and white and ruffled and decorative. I counted eighteen of them before I was interrupted.

"Knock-knock, snacky-wackies are here," said Department Store Mom as she entered the room carrying a silver tray. "The tea is oolong raspberry—organic, of course—which should complement the flavor of the spiced shortbread cookies, which are organic, of course."

"Of course," I said.

"I'll just set this down right here and let you girls be girls. Tee-hee." She giggled and then closed the bedroom door behind her.

I stared.

"What? You don't like shortbread?" asked Beanpole.

"The cookies are shaped like three little schoolgirls holding hands," I commented.

"Yeah," said Beanpole. "Friendship cookies. My mom is big into motifs."

"Motifs?" I said.

"Yep," Beanpole answered with a proud, perky smile. "Motifs."

"Does your mom always do stuff like this for you?" asked Q as she poured herself a cup of tea.

"You mean like making sure I have a balanced snack after school, or folding all my socks and putting them in my dresser drawer according to the height which they'll go up my ankle when I wear them?"

"She does that?" I said.

"Unless I want them color coordinated," Beanpole answered. "Then she'll arrange them according to their hue of brightness."

"Their hue of what?" I said.

"Their hue of brightness," she explained. "You know, light tones on the left, moving through medium colors in the middle, working toward dark shades on the right, ending with black."

"And you find this normal?" I said.

"Uh . . . I never thought about it," she replied.

"Well, think about," I said, reaching for a cookie. "And think hard." I looked at the piece of shortbread I'd picked up.

I looked at Beanpole.

I looked back at the cookie.

One of the girls in the shortbread design was frosted in colors that exactly matched the colors of Beanpole's outfit that day. Beanpole and the cookie were even wearing the same thick, blue belt.

I set the cookie back down. Too spooky.

"Come on, we need an idea," I said, taking out a pencil and notebook to jot down our thoughts. "I mean, what kind of talent are we going to put on for this stupid show?"

"Card tricks?" said Beanpole.

"Do you know any?" I asked, ready to write that down.

"No," she answered. "How about comedy routines?" Beanpole offered.

"Do you know any?" I asked, ready to write that down.

"No," she answered. "How about unicycle riding?" Beanpole offered.

"Do you know how to do that?" I asked, losing my patience.

"No," she answered. "How about magic?" Beanpole offered.

"Do you know any magic?" I said, grinding my teeth.

"No," she answered. "How about . . ."

"Beanpole!" I shouted. "Why do you keep suggesting things that you don't know how to do?"

She paused. "I'm not sure. Just brainstorming, I guess."

"Well, unfortunately, you need a brain to brainstorm!" I turned to Q. "Do you have anything to add to the list? Anything at all? Anything like training a monkey to fly, or creating an underwater opera while dressed as ballet-dancing mermaids? Anything, Q? Anything at all?"

I must have been turning purple with frustration. Q raised her eyebrows, then slowly raised the scuba tank to her lips. *Wheeesh-whooosh. Wheeesh-whooosh.*

"Don't say it," I warned. "Don't say it."

Q cracked a doofy grin. "You're funny."

I threw the paper in the air.

"Oh my gawd, we're terrible!" I shouted. "And we're gonna get trounced! Humiliated. Thoroughly embarrassed! Doesn't it bother either of you that we are the most pathetic creatures in school? Doesn't it bother you one little bit?"

The room fell silent. Neither offered an answer. Finally, after what felt like ten thousand million minutes, Beanpole spoke.

"Wanna know a secret?" she asked softly.

"What, Beanpole," I snapped. "You're growing armpit hair and wanna comb it onstage?" I said. "With your toes, of course?"

"No," she said in an uncharacteristically non-perky tone. "It's just that, well... when I think about girls like the Three-Pees, I just wonder..." She paused. "I just wonder if, ya know, I'm ever gonna have a boyfriend."

I looked up. Silence filled the room.

"I mean, who's ever going to want to be with someone like me?" she said.

I turned to Allergy Alice. She lowered her gaze. I looked back at Beanpole. Sadness filled her eyes.

The room was silent for a whole thirty more seconds. Q took another quiet slurp off her scuba tank.

Wheeesh-whooosh. Wheeesh-whooosh.

Finally, I stood up.

"Well, that's a nice note to end this meeting on. Permanent loneliness." I picked up my backpack. "Can't wait till we meet up tomorrow and figure out another way to make me want to slash my wrists." I headed for the door. "Next meeting is at your house, Q."

"We can't," she answered.

"Why?" I said.

"We just can't," she replied.

"I said, Why?"

"We just can't!" she insisted. And then she started hyperventilating.

Like seriously hyperventilating.

"Alice?" asked Beanpole, the look of concern on her face growing with each hyperventilation. "Alice? Are you okay?"

Q didn't reply.

"Alice?!"

Suddenly, Allergy Alice started desperately gasping for air; her face turned red, then purple, then blue as she sucked and sucked and sucked, but she couldn't seem to get any oxygen.

"Q?" I said. "Q! Quick, call her mom!"

Beanpole rushed for the phone. "I don't know the number."

"Then call nine-one-one!"

Beanpole started to dial.

"No," Q managed to protest through gasps and wheezes and shortness of breath. "Don't."

She looked like she was about to have a seizure.

"Yes, do it!" I shouted at Beanpole. "Don't listen to her. Call!"

Beanpole froze, not knowing what to do. Q dropped to her knees.

"Call!" I shouted again.

"No!" Q shot back. Then she bent over and played doctor to herself.

She interlocked her fingers around her neck and lifted her head up and down in some kind of steady rhythm, and then, even though a moment ago it looked like she was about to have some kind of crazy spasmo attack, she managed to slow down her breathing and get a grip on herself.

In and out, in and out, in and out, her breathing went.

"It's okay. I'll be okay," she said. "Sometimes, I . . . I just get short of breath."

I wasn't sure what to do.

"Do you need your inhaler?" I offered, trying to do something, anything to help.

"No, I just need to walk," she answered.

"Walk?"

Beanpole and I stared, not knowing how to respond. Once Q felt strong enough, she stood up.

"We can't go to my house, okay?" she snapped at me. "We just can't." She picked up her backpack and prepared to leave.

"Where are you going?" I asked.

"Home. I'm walking."

"You're walking?"

She opened the door and made her way out of Beanpole's room. We followed behind her.

"Really, Alice, you should let us call your mom or something," said Beanpole as Q exited through the front door.

"I'll be all right."

"Or let one of our moms drive you," I said.

"I'm not an invalid, you know," she said. "I can walk. Besides, it's the only thing that helps me deal with panic attacks."

Allergy Alice marched down the street without turning around again. Beanpole and I just stood there watching her. I don't think either of us had ever seen Q so angry before.

"What's..." I asked, "...with her?"

"I don't know," said Beanpole. "I don't know."

Q, freak-o that she was, showed up to school the next day as if nothing had happened. Nothing at all. No word about the breathing, no word about the walking, no word about being so angry. She simply set out her garden-grown carrot sticks and container of purple homeopathic beets, and began to eat lunch like there was never a problem in the world.

We even got the same old slurping sounds off the scuba tank every now and then.

Wheeesh-whooosh. Wheeesh-whooosh.

Beanpole and I looked at one another and shrugged. Whatever. If she didn't want to talk about it, we knew she wasn't going to talk about it. Besides, there were bigger fish to fry, like the ThreePees, who just so happened to be practicing a few of their steps on the other side of the courtyard, where, like, the whole school could see.

Wow, were they good.

And even more depressing was that, aside from having an amazing amount of God-given ability, they had professional choreography too. Kiki's mom, we'd just discovered, had hired an ex-NFL cheerleading coach to bring an extra touch of razzle-dazzle to their performance this year.

"I can't believe we don't have our talent yet!" I said.

"Aptitude, remember?" said Beanpole. "It's an aptitude display. Not a talent show."

"Whatever," I replied. Lunch for me today consisted of fruit: blueberries, raspberries, and strawberries.

Otherwise known as berry cobbler.

"So who's our biggest competition?" asked Beanpole. She was eating some sort of quiche made into the shape of the Eiffel Tower.

"You mean aside from the Dallas Cowboys Cheerleaders?" I said.

"Forget them," said Beanpole. Kiki had just done some kind of double backflip that ended in a split. If I tried something like that, there wasn't a pair of pants on this planet that wouldn't split.

"I want to hear who our other competition is," Beanpole said. "Gimme the scoop."

"Right now," answered Q, taking out a sheet of paper with notes scratched all over it, "Mousey Mitchell and Lame Larry are going to do a finger puppet show, Puking Patty Pamplin is going to do some kind of Chinese New Year's dance with scarves...."

"Is Puking Patty Chinese?"

"No, but she's half Irish, and they like to celebrate international culture in her family."

"Go on," said Beanpole.

"The Hammerstrudel triplets are going to do a traditional Dutch dance, and they are going to do it in clogs, but supposedly two of them already have sprained ankles from their practice sessions, so they might not compete."

"Okay, I don't want to hear about every moron in this school," I said. "Just tell me, who's bringing the real heat?"

"Well," said Q, "Four-Eyes Franny supposedly does this mean cup-stacking act. And then, of course, some kids will play the piano, some will sing duets, and Disgusting Danny Dortenfuller, a kid who is really talented, might play the cello, but he broke his finger while picking his nose last week, so he might not compete this year, either."

"How'd he break his finger picking his nose?" I asked.

"Well," said Q, "his father told him to quit eating his boogers, and when he didn't, Disgusting Danny's father smashed his fingers in a door."

"Tough break," I said.

"I guess they don't call him Disgusting Danny for nothin'," said Beanpole.

"And then, of course, there's the ThreePees," said Q, looking over at the girls. "Gymnastics, dance, hip-hop, cheerleading, ballet, and fusion. And you know that ex-NFL coach?" said Q.

"Yeah," I answered.

"Well, their mom hired a lighting technician, too."

"Their own lighting person?" said Beanpole.

"They're gonna have spotlights and special effects and stuff like that," answered Q. "Rumor has it they even got a permit from the fire marshall to create an explosion of some sort for their grand finale."

"Indoor fireworks?"

"It's part of their theme," said Q.

"They have a theme?"

"It's gonna *Rain Gold*. On the audience, that is. With glitter and balloons and stuff."

"Is it just me, or does it seem like they are taking this to a really sick level?" I asked.

"Kiki Masters is living for that yearbook picture right now. She even has a personal trainer. It's the only thing that matters to their family, keepin' their Grover Park streak alive."

"How do you know all this stuff?" I asked.

"I got a special hookup in the nurse's office," said Q. "When I go for my daily shot, she fills me in."

"Your daily shot?" I asked.

Q pretended she didn't hear me, but I knew she did.

"Why do you take a daily shot?" I said, this time loud and clear.

"They're experimental," she answered in a low voice.

"Experimental for what?" I asked.

Allergy Alice raised her head, made eye contact with me, and paused, like she was about to tell me something big. Really big. Like the biggest news a person could ever tell somebody.

"Berries make me sneeze."

"Excuse me?"

"Your berries," she repeated. "They're gonna make me sneeze."

"You want me to throw them out?" I asked.

She thought about it. "Naw. But if you could eat 'em kinda quicker, that might help prevent a few achoos."

"Sure," I said. "Weirdo." I added that last part under my breath. Though I sorta mumbled it, I sorta said it loud enough for her to hear, too.

I munched a bite of food. Q nibbled on a beet. This was one strange girl, I thought. One strange girl. A total and complete question mark.

I looked across the courtyard at the ThreePees. Sofes O'Reilly did a cartwheel that turned into a one-armed handstand. No, she may not have had a brain, but she definitely had a body.

"Aw, I could do that," said Beanpole, standing up to prove it wasn't so hard. Then she tripped over her backpack and smashed into a pole.

"Ouch!" she said. "Don't worry, I'm okay. I'm okay."

When she came back over, my eyes almost bugged out.

"Oh my goodness," I said. "Beanpole, your pinkie finger is like totally bending in the wrong direction."

"What?" she said, wiping some dirt off her knee. "Oh, that?" she replied casually. "I'm double-jointed."

And with that she twisted her finger back into place as if it were on some sort of swivel.

"I have a rib that pops out, too. Wanna see?" she eagerly asked, beginning to lift her shirt.

"No," I said, grabbing her. "I don't."

"All right," she said, disappointed that I didn't want to see another one of her human freak-ball abilities.

"I can also pick up a cordless telephone with my knees," she offered.

I ignored the comment. With the ThreePees already look-ing like yearbook champions, and us a completely lost mess of a group, I realized that I needed to take charge of this situation before it ended up a total disaster.

Or at least a total disaster more than it already was a total disaster.

"Okay, here's the deal," I said with firmness in my voice. "We'll meet again at my house today after school."

I paused and slowly turned my head toward Allergy Alice.

"That would be my house, right, Q?"

She didn't answer. All I got was a *Wheeesh-whooosh. Wheeesh-whooosh.*

"Four fifteen," I added. "Be there and be prepared for greatness!"

With that, I picked up my stuff and walked away.

Of course, I didn't have any greatness planned. I didn't even have any terribleness planned. There wasn't a thing in the world I could think of that would even give us a shot at taking down the ThreePees. Not a dang thing.

When Q and Beanpole arrived, we went straight to my room.

"So whaddya we got?" I asked, my mouth full of Oreos. This time I was the one who brought the plate of cookies into the room, but Q and Beanpole were still skeptical. I had to eat three of them before either would dare to take a taste.

"So," began Beanpole, twisting open a cookie and licking out the frosting. I could tell by the way she barely tapped the edge of the cookie cream with her tongue that she was still worried about ending up with her taste buds covered in fluoride protec-tion. "After you left, Alice and I came up with some stuff."

"Talk to me," I said.

"We could invent fire."

"You're about four thousand years too late."

"We could levitate."

"Do I even need to respond to that?"

"Okay," she said, checking off items on the sheet of paper in her hand. "Then I guess I don't need to mention the challenge-the-audience-to-a-blindfolded-arm-wrestling-contest-over-a pit-of-alligators idea either."

I shook my head. "No, I don't think you do."

"That means we're down to either not being able to solve a giant-sized Rubik's Cube puzzle or doing some sort of white belt tae kwan do."

"White belt tae kwan do?" I asked. "What's that?"

"Well, instead of breaking a board or a concrete block with the power of our fists, we would smash through some paper towels."

"Paper towels?"

"Yeah, pre-wetted ones. Unless you think pre-wetted napkins would make the karate moves look more impressive," answered Beanpole. "I'm not sure people in the audience would be able to see the difference, though, especially in the back, so we might be able to get away with one here."

"Oh yes," I said in a tone dripping with sarcasm. "Napkins for sure. I mean what kind of jujitsu masters would we be if we didn't rise to the challenge of smashing through a pre-wetted paper napkin."

I could tell Beanpole understood that I thought these were some of the stupidest ideas I'd ever heard.

"There's always my earwax thing," she offered. "It's why I never fail to carry Q-tips with me, just in case anyone ever wants to see it."

Just then, Beanpole pulled out a Q-tip out of her sock. I glared. Being a minor, and clearly being provoked, I doubted the courts would give me much more than second-degree manslaughter for the elimination of this person from our species. Heck, I'd probably be out of the big house in time for high school graduation.

"I'm telling ya, it's impressive," she continued.

Suddenly, there was a knock at my door. Thank goodness, too. It just may have saved Beanpole's life. I answered politely.

"Go away!"

They knocked again.

"I said, Go away!" I repeated as I stood to deliver the message face-to-face. If it was Ashley, I was gonna pound her face into pecan pie.

I threw open the door. It was Marty. Beanpole and Q jumped backward and immediately flinched. Q's hands rose. She instinctively covered her ears.

"Relax. I'm here to help," he said.

"Shove off, butthead," I said, trying to shut the door in my brother's face, but he stuck his foot in the door crack so I couldn't close it.

"I said, I'm hear to help," he repeated. "Can't you just trust me for one minute?"

I looked at Beanpole and Q.

"Nope."

"Nuh-uh."

"No way."

It was the one of the only times the three of us had ever been in agreement about anything.

"Just trust me," said Marty, forcing his way into my room. "I've got a plan to help you win the talent show."

We paused and stared at one another. With words like those, how could we not at least listen?

arty led us into the garage. To the black bags. Q was shaking the whole way.

"Relax," said Marty in the maturest-sounding, sixteen-year-old voice he could speak in. "I have allergies too."

"Ya do?" I said. I never knew that.

"To dogs," continued Marty. He started to open one of the black bags—one that was buried deep in the back of all the garage junk. "And my dad, well, he was going to make me one. Build me a dog."

"Build you a dog?" asked Beanpole, not quite following.

"Yeah, he was kinda this mad professor type," said Marty. "Always building weird stuff. Odd things, ya know, created just to sort of have a good time. Not much value to anyone, but fun. Guess I kinda take after him."

Marty opened the bag, realized it was not the one he was looking for, then grabbed another one.

"Yep, this is it," he said as he opened it. We looked inside.

All it really seemed like was a bunch of mechanical crazy parts and stuff. I didn't see where this was going.

"This is stupid," I said. "Let's get out of here before we end up having our teeth turned pink or something."

"Just wait a sec, will ya?" Marty said, pulling out a few random pieces. "At first I was just gonna kinda make it for you, but then I realized you don't need my help making it. You can build it yourself. All the things are here. You just need me to fix the central programming system, the brain, but you can put it all together yourself."

"You want us to make a dog? For the talent show?" I said. "That is so stupid. You really are a butthead."

"Not just make a dog," he answered. "But bring it onstage with you. This dog can bark, walk on its head, do tricks.... It'll be like a twenty-first-century demonstration of talent."

"Aptitude," said Beanpole, clarifying.

"Whatever," said Marty. "Aptitude."

I looked over, thinking, Can we just get out of here already? But Beanpole and Q seemed intrigued.

"Instead of you just being lame dancers, this dog can be the dancer. You can work out a whole routine around it."

"You mean like our talent will be to give the dog talent?" said Q.

"Exactly," answered Marty.

"But then it's not really our abilities, it's yours," I said. "We'll get disqualified."

"I doubt it," he answered. "I mean, the Masters sisters and

their mom are fully choreographing, planning, designing the outfits and the fireworks spectacular for their sister, right? I think you can accept a little help from your brother, don't you?"

I looked at him with a sideways glare.

Skeptical. Highly skeptical.

"Look, you come up with the ideas, you work out the routine, you plan it all out, and I'll make this pooch spin on its tail if you want."

Q and Beanpole looked at one another. They seemed to be seriously considering it.

"My mom could knit us sweaters," said Beanpole.

"I bet she could," I answered.

"And we could be, like, color coordinated with matching hair bands," Beanpole added.

"Oh, really? Could we?" I said, clapping my hands together in a peppy way. "Oh, joy."

"Well, I'm kinda good with a screwdriver and a wrench," said Q, showing a bit of interest. "I mean, if that's all it takes to put this thing together."

"Aside from the computer brain, it's just a matter of turning some screws and tightening some bolts," said my brother.

"Can it really dance?" asked Beanpole.

"It'll do a Tuscan tango if you want," he answered.

Beanpole started to get perky. "Well, even I know how to operate a screwdriver," she said, grabbing a Phillips-head screwdriver that was sitting on a nearby shelf.

Of course, when she grabbed the screwdriver she knocked over a hammer... which fell on her foot.

"Ouch!" she yelped. "Don't worry, don't worry. I'm okay."

"Who's worried?" I asked.

Q picked up two pieces from the bag of parts and started exploring how they might fit together.

"Wait a sec," I said. "How do I know this isn't some practical joke that's gonna blow up onstage and make me look like an idiot in front of everybody?" I asked Marty.

"It won't," he answered.

"But how do I know?" I said. "Like why are you doing this?"

Marty paused. For the first time ever, I saw a piece of a real human being inside of him.

"Because I hate dad for leaving us just as much as you do, Maureen," he answered. "And when I think about how many times I needed a father to help me out, to show me how something worked, or how much he hurt Mom, well..." He stopped. "I hate his guts."

Ouch. We all fell silent. Marty had gotten really deep all of a sudden.

"Besides," he said, stopping himself before he allowed any tears to fall from his eyes. "You see this trophy?" He pulled something out of an old, dusty cabinet. "Second Place," he said. "Back when I was at Grover Park, I was robbed. It should have been first, and all I ever thought about the rest of that year was how someone needed to put CeCe 'The Cheater' Masters in her place. Bunch of witches in that family."

We all laughed.

"I mean, when it comes to payback, better late than never, right?" said Marty, looking at the bag of robotic dog parts.

We stared at one another.

"So, whaddya think?" Marty asked.

"It's better than nothing," Beanpole said.

"And nothing's all we got," added Q.

There was another pause while we thought about it.

"And maybe I could, like, get the wax out of its ears or something?" added Beanpole.

"With your toe?" I said.

"With my toe," she answered.

I shook my head. Q reached back into the bag and fumbled
around.

"Wheels for feet?" she asked Marty.

"And a tail with a stopper so it can stand and spin."

Q rummaged through more parts.

"I could do this," she said. "I could put this together."

"And let me tell you," Marty added, "by the time I am done
with the programming, this dog will be able to bark, wiggle,
heck... I can make it lick its crotch if you want. I figured out
how to program all sorts of moves from this Web site I found."

Beanpole looked at me with a serious expression. "Mo,
you realize, if this robot dog actually does half the things your
brother says, and we, like, plan this big, funny, awesome routine,
we might win. We might win the whole darn thing."

I look at the black bag, then raised my gaze.

"Not *might* win, Beanpole," I answered with a steel look in
my eyes. "We're gonna win."

Marty smiled.

Beanpole smiled.

Q, well, she just took a suck off the scuba tank. *Wheeesh-whoosh. Wheeesh-whoosh.* Then she got that Wild West gun-fighter look in her eyes.

"Better watch your backsides, ThreePees...." said Q. *Wheeesh-whooosh. Wheeesh-whoosh.* " 'Cause here come the Nerd Girls."

Turns out that Q was pretty good with tools. Unfortunately, Beanpole was not.

"Ouch!" she yelped. "Don't worry, don't worry. I'm okay, I'm okay." I heard that phrase so many times while we were in the garage building the dog, I stopped even bothering to find out how Beanpole had hurt herself.

"Who's worried?" I said.

Q took a slurp off the scuba tank—*Wheeesh-whoosh. Wheeesh-whooosh*—then used a ratchet to tighten an interior screw near the dog's upper thigh.

"Pass me that power drill, would you?" said Q, pointing at the tool shelf.

"You know how to use a power drill?" I said.

"Yeah, my dad taught me," she answered. I passed her the power tool, and she thoughtfully looked through the drill bits, searching for the right size. "I think I wanna bolt his tail from the underside in order to make sure it can hold up his entire weight when we get to the spin part. Just to reinforce it, ya know?"

"Uh, yeah," I answered. "Whatever you say."

Every time I thought I was getting a grip on this girl, Q pulled out something new on me, something completely out of nowhere. Like I said, a total question mark.

"Maybe we should shape the ears into cute little stars," said Beanpole, holding a saw. "Like sparkly, diamondy ones," she added.

A saw?!

I leaped for the instrument before Beanpole cut off her arm.

"I think we better leave the big-girl tools to the big girls," I said, taking away the blade. "Here, take a pen and start jotting down a list of possible doggie names. Pens are safe."

"But I want to saw."

"Beanpole, even though amputating your head might not be a bad thing for the rest of humanity, I don't want to have to clean up all the blood." I picked up a yellow legal pad. "Besides, we have to call this robotic thingy something. Make a list and then we'll let you paint the dog's name on the side of its body once we choose something. Cool?"

I passed her the pen.

"Start with ten names, narrow it down to five, and then come back to us with your top three."

Beanpole took the pen and paper and crossed the garage to come up with a name. I knew she was disappointed about not being able to saw, but I also knew she realized I was probably right. Bruises were one thing; missing body parts were something else all together.

I walked back over to Q just as she squeezed the trigger of the drill to test it out.

"So what's your dad do?" I asked. The drill made a louder *veeezz-veeezz* sound.

"What'd you say?" She hadn't heard me over the noise.

"Ouch! I poked myself with the pen," came a cry from across the room. There was a pause. "Don't worry, don't worry. I'm okay, I'm okay."

Q and I shook our heads and laughed.

"Your dad," I repeated. "What's he do?"

The expression on Q's face suddenly changed to a blank, pale stare.

"Q?" I said. "Your father? What's he do?" I repeated.

Yeesh, just when I thought this girl might actually be starting to flash signs of normalcy, out came ol' wacko again.

Q turned her head and stared off into nothingness. Suddenly she began to wheeze.

"Q?" I said.

She didn't answer.

"Q?" I said again. "You okay?"

And then, just like last time, she began to seriously hyperventilate. I couldn't believe how quickly things had gone from really calm to really intense.

Q wheezed and sucked and gasped for air like she was a person on the moon who wasn't wearing a space suit. A moment later she dropped to her knees and started doing that weird rhythm breathing stuff again.

In and out and in and out.

I stood over her, unsure of what to do.

In and out and in and out.

"Q?"

She didn't reply.

"Q, are you..."

"I need to..." she gasped. "Go for a walk."

"A walk?" I asked. "You need to go for a walk right now?"

She stood up.

"Walking...it helps calm me down," she said between desperate breaths. "Gotta go walk."

She left the drill where it was, she left the dog where it was, she left me where I was. No explanation. No good-bye. No anything. She just grabbed her backpack and went for a walk.

I stood there stunned. *What in the world?* A minute later Beanpole came over.

"So whaddya think of the name...drumroll please... Poochy?"

I didn't answer. I just stared in dumb silence.

"What, you don't like it?" she asked. "I think it's kinda good. Hey, where's Alice?"

"She, uh...left," I said. "Had to go for a walk."

"A walk?" said Beanpole with a puzzled look on her face.

"Yeah. Said she needed to calm herself down."

"What'd you say to her?"

"Nothing," I said.

Beanpole rolled her eyes and gave me an I-totally-don't-believe-you look.

"I swear, nothing," I repeated. "I didn't say anything. And stop looking at me like that. I can be nice, you know, you klutz-face dork-o-rama!"

I put down the bolts I was holding and looked at the robotic dog. Marty had been working on the brain on his own time in his room, and while I had turned a few screws and twisted a few parts, Q was the one who had really assembled most of our project. And made a bunch of improvements, too. Without her, I don't know where we would have been.

I bent down and began to put all the various things away.

"Come on, Beanpole, let's clean this stuff up."

Beanpole bent down to help.

"Ouch! I bumped my head. Don't worry, don't worry. I'm okay."

I took a deep breath.

"Lord help the insurance company that covers you," I said, reaching for the bag where all the stuff went.

"Insurance company? Why?" said Beanpole. "Ouch! I smashed my hand. Don't worry, don't worry. I'm okay."

"Try not to break the dog, Beanpole," I said. "You, I'm not so worried about. But the dog, it's all we got."

"You mean Poochy." Beanpole smiled big and proud.

"Yeah, Poochy," I said. "Just be careful."

Of course, the next day at school Q showed up with her detoxified, desalinated, deflavored lunch and didn't say a stinking word about the previous day. She just acted like always, as if nothing had happened. She simply ate her peeled tomato skin, tree bark, and tofu salad as if life was as normal as ever.

Wheeesh-whooosh. Wheeesh-whooosh.

"Tell me," I said. "Why do you need that tank again?"

"I take medicine."

"And you take medicine because…"

"Because I am sick," she answered.

"And you are sick with an illness that..."

"Needs medicine," she replied.

"Which is why you slurp off a tank," I said, completing her sentence.

"Exactly," she answered. "You got it."

"Oh good, I got it," I said. "I don't understand anything, but I got it."

What a freak-a-zoid, I thought.

I would have said something more. I really was going to, but I had bigger problems that day. Mr. Piddles, in all his social studies wisdom, had teamed every member in his second period class with a partner to do a "Justice Project."

And I got teamed with Logan Meyers. Of all people.

"So what's the problem?" asked Beanpole when I told her of my dilemma. Lunch today for her was homemade lasagna shaped in the form of a Baroque cathedral. "We know you like him."

My heart dropped.

"I do not," I said, acting casual.

"Do too," answered Beanpole, smiling and happy she had some inside scoop on me. "It's like so obvious, Maureen."

"I do not," I said again, working as hard as I could to remain calm.

I looked at Q. She sucked on the scuba tank.

Wheeesh-whooosh. Wheeesh-whooosh.

But I could tell by the way she slurped, she was sending me a message that said, yeah, she knew too.

"I do not!" I insisted.

"Do too."

"Do not!"

"Do too."

The three of us looked across the courtyard. Logan was standing on a chair, balancing on one foot and pretending to sniff his armpits.

I tried not to drool. He was just, like, *soooooooooooo* hot.

"I wonder if he's a good kisser?" asked Q.

"What?" I said, spinning around.

"A good kisser," she repeated. "I mean, just because he's good-looking doesn't mean he's a good kisser, you know."

"Make sure you tell us when you tongue him, Maureen," said Beanpole.

"When I do what?" I said. My jaw practically dropped to the floor. Q laughed.

"I heard he tongued Kiki Masters," said Beanpole. "Twice." My eyes narrowed, and I shot her a fierce look. "Just warnin' ya," she added.

"Well, I heard Kiki Masters tongued Justin Barnes," added Q. "And Mitchell Welton, too."

I rolled my eyes.

"By the time she graduates, who won't Kiki have tongued?" I snipped. "Every boy in Grover Park Middle School will probably have had a spit sample off the girl."

We laughed and then turned to look over at the ThreePees, who were, of course, practicing their amazing routine for all the world to see.

We watched for a minute. Holy macaroni they were good.

Just then, as the ThreePees were razzle-dazzling, Sofes O'Reilly turned left when she was supposed to turn right, and threw the whole routine off.

Kiki stopped mid-dance. Just stopped. Then she shot Sofes a furious glare. I could feel the heat of her anger from across the courtyard.

"Um, hello?" snapped Kiki. She stormed to their table and shut off the music. "Like, do you know your left from your right?"

"Uh, yeah," said Sofes.

"Prove it," said Kiki.

"Excuse me?"

"I said, 'Prove it,'" snapped Kiki as she put her hand on her hip and gave Sofes a mean glare. "Prove to me right now that you know your left from your right."

A bunch of people stared.

"Like, um, you're embarrassing me, Keeks," Sofes said softly.

"Like, it's, um, embarrassing that you can't do one simple turn on an eight count," answered Kiki in a mean, sarcastic tone.

"Geez, I just made a mistake," said Sofes, more to Brittany-Brattany than anyone else.

Brittany-Brattany, always the courageous one, stood up for Sofes by lowering her eyes and not saying a word.

Kiki walked back over to the music player.

"Well, maybe it was a mistake to bring you on the team," said Kiki, getting ready to take it from the top once again. "Maybe we shouldda left you in Loserville."

"Like, um, harsh," said Sofes.

"Like, um, true," answered Kiki.

Brittany-Brattany remained silent.

"Oh my gawd," said Beanpole, back over at our table. "Like I just have absolutely no idea what boys see in her at all. Not at all."

Just then, Kiki took off her sweatshirt. Underneath her loose-fitting hoodie she wore a skintight, lycra, low-cut tank top that revealed more curves than any road in the city.

"They see those," said Q. "Both of 'em."

Q raised the scuba tank to her lips and took a big suck. *Wheeesh-whooosh. Wheeesh-whooosh.*

Then the three of us laughed so loud, everyone in the court-yard looked over to see what was funny. I just covered my mouth and giggled some more.

Wow, Q made a funny.

12

Who's ready for some snacky-wackies?" said Department Store Mom as she carried a tray of freshly baked scones into Beanpole's bedroom. "I've got Academy Awards today. Organic, of course."

I looked at the scones, and sure enough they had been crafted into little gold Oscar statuettes, just like the kind they give to all the movie people when they win an Academy Award. Department Store Mom's theme today was Show Business Victory. She was trying to make sure we stayed inspired for the big competition next week.

"Mmm, these are delicious, Mrs. Tanner," said Q after taking a bite. "Thank you." No need to worry about dental hygiene products being placed in your food in this house. Department Store Mom was a great cook, and once she'd learned about all of Q's special dietary needs, she'd taken it as a personal baking challenge to make one hundred percent nonallergenic after-school treats for us that were one hundred percent tasty and delicious. And I have to say, the stuff she was coming up with was amazing. The woman could have opened a bakery.

"Great job, Mommy," said Beanpole, biting the head off a statuette. "And the sweaters, I saw them downstairs. They look awesome!"

"Oh, you did?" said Department Store Mom with a whole bunch of perkiness. Like it was really hard to tell where Beanpole got all her zing. "I was going to bring them up for sizing if you girls were ready today."

"Uh, yeah."

"Sure," I said, but the words *sweaters* and *sizing* together made me feel instantly uncomfortable. I knew this day would come, though. Had known it for a while now.

"Great. I'll be back with more tea and the outfits for the big show in a jiff." Department Store Mom backed out of the room and disappeared down the hall, not a thread of carpet disturbed by any step the woman ever took.

Totally weird.

Actually, I was kinda feeling the good vibes in Beanpole's house as of late, and Department Store Mom's Department Store Mom-ness wasn't really getting on my nerves so much anymore. After all, she had knitted matching sweaters for the three of us —plus one for Poochy, the robotic dog—and every time we came over she was just so ridiculously nice it was hard to hate her.

I tried, though, I have to admit. But I just couldn't.

"Hey, sporto, how's the talent practice going?" said

Department Store Dad, coming in to give his daughter a peck on her cheek. He was another one I wanted to not like, but couldn't. Just too nice and friendly.

"Hi, girls," he said, giving Q and me a white, smiley, glow-bright flash of teeth.

"Hi, Mr. Tanner," said Q.

"Nice sweater," I commented.

"Oh, you like?" he answered. "I was in the mood for checkers today."

"Looks sharp on you," I said. "Not everyone can get away with wearing those, you know."

"Well, thank you, Maureen," he answered. "Oh, sporto," Department Store Dad added, "don't forget about the family portrait we're gonna take the night before the show. I wanna make sure we have a professional photographer get a good shot of us. You know, for the mantel."

So that's where those photos came from when you bought picture frames at a department store. Beanpole's family posed for them.

"Got it, Daddy," she said.

"You're the best, princess. Bye, girls."

"Bye," we said, and with another white smile, Department Store Dad left to go trim a hedge or something.

"Don't you want a scone, Mo?" asked Beanpole.

"Um, no thanks," I answered softly, lowering my eyes. My face kinda flushed.

Beanpole and Q looked up, wondering what was wrong. Usually I was good for at least half a plate of baked treats washed down by three cups of tea with extra sugar.

"I'm sort of trying to, you know, watch what I eat," I added.

The room got quiet. Real quiet. I expected them to laugh at me. My whole life people had laughed at me about my weight.

But the laughter never came.

"Good for you," said Beanpole, full of perk. "I mean, I think you're pretty just the way you are, but it's important to feel good about yourself."

"You have nice skin," said Q.

"What?" I said.

"Your skin," she answered. "It's nice. I have pimples and acne and stuff, but you . . . you have nice skin."

"Oh," I said. I'd never really thought about my skin. I guess it was kinda clear compared to some other kids. "Um, thanks."

"Sure," said Q.

Just then, Department Store Mom burst back into the room with an arm full of pink sweaters. "Guess whose sweaty-whetties are here," she said, unable to contain her excitement. "This one's for Alice." She handed Q a sweater. "This one's for Maureen," she said, passing me mine. "And this one is for Barbara. Go ahead, try them on. Let's see how they look."

Department Store Mom put her hands on her hips and waited to see how her master works would fit us.

The three of us froze.

Try them on?

Gulp.

"Is something wrong?" asked Department Store Mom, like totally not getting it. Or maybe she had forgotten what it was like to be our age. I mean, did she really want us to take off our shirts in front of one another? That would involve breasts!

Suddenly, the lightbulb went off in Department Store Mom's head. "Oh," she said. "Of course." Her tone was warm and understanding. "There's a bathroom right down the hall. How about if you go in one at a time and change?"

We breathed a deep sigh of relief.

"You know, I used to face this all the time when I managed the department store. Young girls can be sensitive about their bodies, but don't worry about it. One at a time is just fine."

"Wait a minute," I said, interrupting. "You used to work at a department store?"

"Oh yeah," Beanpole's mom answered. "For years. I tell you," she said with a fond smile, "once that job gets in your blood, it's hard to get it out."

She laughed as she took a quick stroll down memory lane.

Weird, I thought. Totally weird.

We went to the bathroom, one at a time. Beanpole was first. Her sweater was tight and showed everything. Or everything that wasn't there. I mean, they didn't call her Beanpole for nothing. But the sweater fit well and looked sharp, that was for sure.

"Feels great, Mom."

"You were easy," said Department Store Mom. "Alice... you're next."

I'm not sure how how Department Store Mom had done it, but when Alice put on that sweater, it fit perfectly. I mean, perfectly. It's like the Department Store Mom had a sixth sense about sizing or something. Like, she had never even measured us.

"This tone really brings out your color well," said Department Store Mom to Allergy Alice as she tugged at the sides of the sweater to make sure that it fit properly. "And the V-neck is a good cut for you," she added.

"You think so?" said Q.

"Oh yeah," said Department Store Mom. "Makes you look tall and proud."

"I don't really wear V-necks," said Q. "You know, 'cause of the scar."

Q pulled the sweater about an inch to the right and revealed a bubbly, craggly, long, deep, really-painful-to-get type of scar.

"I usually hide it by wearing tops with high necks and stuff," she said. We could tell she was embarrassed.

Beanpole and I looked at one another. It was the first time we had seen or heard about any scar, but Department Store Mom just rolled right with it as if it were no big deal at all.

"Now, let's see," said Department Store Mom, staring at Q while contemplating a way to work some magic. "We have a couple of options." She paused for a moment. "I got it. How about if I get everyone some tank tops for underneath the sweaters? That way it would still leave a low neckline but would keep this part covered for each of you, kind of like a little optical illusion."

Q looked over at me and Beanpole with hopeful eyes as Department Store Mom sized up the type of tank tops to get.

"Could you, Mommy?" said Beanpole. "I mean, I'd wear one," she added. They all looked at me.

"Uh, yeah," I said. "Of course. Sure, I'll wear it," I said. "And since you're creating optical illusions, can you do anything to, you know, make me look like less of a baked potato?"

Everyone laughed.

"Well, it's true, isn't it?" I said. "My body looks like something that should be served with steak and salad."

They laughed again.

"I tell you what," said Department Store Mom. "We'll make the tank tops black. Dark tones slenderize, you know."

"They do?" I said.

"Oh yeah," said Department Store Mom. "See, the key to being a good dresser is accents and misdirection. You want to accent the things you want to show, and kind of misdirect attention away from the parts you want to conceal."

"Oh my goodness," I said, suddenly feeling happy. "I'm never going to wear anything lighter than pitch black again. People are going to think I'm Miss Halloween."

They all chuckled.

"You can wear colors, Maureen," said Department Store Mom. "And there are some other tricks I can show you, too."

"Really?" I said.

"Oh yeah," she answered. "Wait till I show you scarves and high belts and things," she added. "I'm the queen of accessories."

"Oh no," said Beanpole with a laugh. "Don't get my mother started on accessories. We'll end up having to have a sleepover tonight."

The four of us chuckled. Actually, it didn't sound like that bad of an idea, but it was a school night and sleepovers aren't really that good on school nights.

"Wait till you see my mommy's closet," added Beanpole. "It's like an outlet store in there."

I turned and looked at myself in the full-length mirror. I'd been wearing baggy clothes for so long, clothes that made me look like a marshmallow, that I had totally missed the boat on realizing how much stuff that fit me well could actually flatter me.

Gee, I thought as I turned and looked at my butt, I look kinda cute.

Though I would never say it, of course.

I walked into my house later that afternoon, floating on clouds. There was just something so nice about seeing how really close Beanpole was with her mom. And when I saw Q's mom come pick her up later that day, the first thing I noticed was how she kissed her daughter's head and fussed over her as if she were the most important thing in the world. Both of them were really lucky to have such good relationships with their moms.

I wanted to be lucky and have a good relationship with my mom, too.

"Mom," I said as I walked into the living room, where she was trying to balance the checkbook. When Grandpa passed, he'd left my mom everything, and while we weren't millionaires, my mom had enough.

"Yeah, Boo," she answered without looking up.

"Do you wanna go grocery shopping?" I asked.

My mom froze.

"Grocery shopping?" she said, turning to stare at me to see if I felt all right. "But you never want to go grocery shopping, Boo. You hate grocery shopping."

"Well, I . . ." I was a bit embarrassed to say anything. "Well, I kinda want to get some stuff. You know, some fruits and vegetables and stuff."

My mom set down her pen. I think she knew where I was going with this.

"Boo, I would love to go grocery shopping with you. Let me get my keys."

Just then, Ashley walked into the room, head down, text messaging on her phone.

"Where ya goin'?" she asked.

"Grocery shopping with Boo," she answered.

"Maureen is going to the supermarket?" Ashley said with her usual sarcasm. "What, is there an eight-for-one sale on chocolate fudge cake?"

Rip! Grab! Smash!

Suddenly my mother tore the phone out of Ashley's hand and slammed it to the ground. The battery popped out and bits of plastic went flying. Right in the middle of Ashley sending a text message, too.

Ashley looked up, stunned and silent.

"No one likes a brat, dear," said my mother in a calm, even voice. "Come on, Boo. Get your jacket."

And with that we walked out the door.

I followed along, knowing that my mom fully expected Ashley to clean up every last bit of broken phone before we got back to the house. I was also sure that it would be at least a month before Ashley would get up the nerve to ask Mom for a new cellie. After a month, of course, of behaving like a total and complete angel. Dang, Ashley has screwed up BIG-TIME!

I jumped into the car, fastened my seat belt, and we pulled out of the driveway.

"After three kids, I've got a set of hips that need their own Zip code," said my mom, breaking the silence. "Maybe we could do some protein shakes or something together?"

"Protein shakes?" I said. "But, Mom, you're not fat."

"Yeah, well, when you get to be my age, who couldn't stand to drop a few, right?" she said. "Me and you, we can do this together."

I looked over. There were tears in my mother's eyes. It was the first time since the night my father ran out on her that I'd seen her cry.

"You know, maybe, if you want, we can try to get into shape together," she added.

These weren't sad tears, though. These were tears of love. Tears of love for me.

"That'd be cool, Mom," I said. "Mother-daughter protein shakes sound like a good idea."

Mom wiped her eyes and smiled.

"Then it's a plan," she said. "But God, I hope they have chocolate," she added. "I don't know if life is worth living without chocolate."

We laughed. Even though Mom was driving, I slid over so I could sit really close to her. My dad might have been a total loser, a complete no-show in my life, but sometimes a great mom could make up for it a thousand times over.

13

Putting on the sweater that Department Store Mom had made for me showed me that maybe I wasn't the ugliest, most worthless, pathetic creature to ever ooze across the planet. In a way, it got things rolling. After all, I'd walked three days in a row with my mom before school, avoided all sort of sweets and pit stops at the Paradise Palace, and had protein shakes—chocolate flavored, of course—twice a day.

"Diet and exercise, that's the key, Boo," said my mom as we finished a mile and a half walk-and-jog mixture around the neighborhood that had started at five-thirty a.m. "Fruits and vegetables, diet and exercise, watch the sugar. That's the key."

Though I had probably only lost about two and a half ounces so far, I felt better about myself and wasn't so ashamed about doing things like getting up in the middle of class and crossing the room to sharpen my pencil. Skinny people never think about stuff like that. But pudgies like me do. All our lives.

"I have to pee," I said at lunch, sitting at our usual table, far away from the other humanoids.

"You just went," said Beanpole.

"I know," I answered, popping a no calorie, pine-flavored mint into my mouth. "But I'm trying to hydrate, so I'm drinking all this water, and it's running right through me."

"Maybe you've got a bladder tumor," offered Beanpole.

I glared.

"What?" she said. "People get bladder tumors all the time."

"I don't have a bladder tumor," I said.

"Maybe you have a urinary tract infection," Beanpole said.

I glared again.

"What?" she said. "People get urinary tract infections all the time."

"I don't have a urinary tract infection," I said.

"Maybe your kidneys are deformed."

"Maybe your brain is deformed!" I snapped. "Maybe the stork only delivered half a package to your mom's house when you were born, and right now there's a head flying around in the sky without a neck to put it on." I picked up my stuff. "I'll see ya tomorrow," I said. "We can continue working on Poochy then."

"We're not meeting today?" asked Beanpole.

"Like, how could you not remember?" answered Q. "Today is Mo's first after-school meeting with"—*Wheeesh-whooosh. Wheeesh-whooosh*—"the Greek god of middle school boys."

"I never shouldda told you that," I said, popping another mint into my mouth.

"But you did."

"But I shouldn't have."

"But you did."

"But I shouldn't have."

"But you did," said Q.

"You're a doofus," I replied. "That was a secret."

"My mom thinks we oughtta keep Poochy a secret," said Beanpole. "She thinks that since no one really knows what we're doing right now, we can use the element of surprise to our advantage."

"My lips are sealed," I said, picking up my backpack.

"Don't seal 'em too much," said Q. "You won't be able to *smoochy-smoochy* Logan if you do." She pretended to wrap a big hug around an imaginary boy and *smoochy-smoochy* him with tongue and everything.

"Very funny, dorkasaurus," I said, walking away. "And by the way, this whole sense-of-humor thing you got going on these days, it's not really working for me. I think I liked you better as a hermit, no personality, a freak-a-zoid."

"Be sure to tell us when you give him a hickey!" Q replied, making more *smoochy-smoochy* sounds.

"You're"—I pretended to be Q and made a loud scuba tank sucking sound—"*Wheeesh-whooosh. Wheeesh-whooosh.* FUN-NEEEE! *Wheeesh-whooosh. Wheeesh-whooosh.*" I made the most cross-eyed, exaggerated doofus face I could to go along with my scuba-slurping impersonation.

Then I stopped and froze. My sucking-off-the-scuba-tank sound was so way over the top, and with all of the exaggeration, well... for a sec I thought I had gone too far.

Like way too far.

Then Q laughed.

"You're a nerd," she said.

Phew, she wasn't mad.

"Look who's talking," I answered.

"Have a good first date," she replied.

"It's not a date," I said. "It's business. It's all business."

"Yeah, the business of *smoochy-smoochy*," she replied.

I walked away, nervous. So nervous. Especially about my breath. I was so concerned about having a mouth that tasted like the butt of Dracula that I had started sucking on breath mints every half hour for the past four days. Today I was up to one breath freshener every eleven minutes. I'd even set my alarm last night to wake up at 2:45 a.m. in order to suck six Tic Tacs. I know that may sound stupid, but when it came to breath and boys, could a girl ever be too concerned?

Logan and I had planned to meet in the library at 3:45. I showed up nineteen minutes and twenty-eight seconds early. Logan showed up fourteen minutes and thirty-seven seconds late. Not that I was keeping track or anything.

"Hi," I said enthusiastically when he appeared. I gave the *H* in *Hi* some extra punch. After sixteen mints, four mouth-wash rinses, and two school bathroom tooth brushings (don't ask what it's like to scrub your chompers in the Grover Park Middle School girls' bathroom. One word: boogersinthesink. *Gross!*), my breath was pine-tree fresh.

"Hey," he answered, taking a seat. Me, I had three note-books, four pens, a rainbow assortment of highlighters, and two pages worth of project ideas ready to go before we even began.

Logan hadn't even brought his backpack.

"Projects are stupid," he said.

"Yeah-*HUHH*!" I said blowing a big *H* his way so that he could get a whiff of the smell-niceness on my breath. I fluttered my eyes.

"And school is stupid," he said.

"Yeah-*HUHH*!" I agreed, punctuating the thought with another *H* full of freshness. My mouth tasted like pine trees, and my breath, I was sure it was going to make him think of mountain ranges and fresh powdered snow and eating perfectly purple, round grapes off my bare neck in a bubbling, hot tub Jacuzzi.

With wild elk in the distance!

I mean, ya gotta have wild elk, right?

"And teachers are stupid too," he said.

"Yeah-*HUHH*!" I said. "They sure are-*HUHH*!"

"Are you all right?" he asked.

"Um, sure. Sure-*huhh*," I said, slipping in one more pine-flavored *H*. For the elk, of course.

"I like video games," he told me. "They're not stupid."

"No-*huhh*," I responded, sending a wind tunnel his way. "Not stupid at all-*huhh*."

"I mean, even the stupid ones aren't stupid," he said. "Not stupid like school."

"Care for a mint-*huhh*?" I said, reaching into my back-pack to offer Logan a taste of enchanted forest. "They're pine flavored-*huhh*."

"Nah, I hate pine," he said. "Smell of it makes me think of nature and the woods and stuff. I hate the woods. The woods are stupid."

"O," I said, careful not to add an *H*. I quickly put away the mints. "I ate the woods too."

"You ate the woods?"

"I...um..." *Gulp. Quick, must think, must think.* "I...um ...greatly dislike the woods, that's what I mean." Though I had practiced in my head quickly, I was pretty sure there were no *H* sounds in the words *greatly dislike*.

I searched around for an ashtray to lick or glass of sour milk to suck down to get the stupid pine flavor off my tongue. *Gawd*, how could I be so idiotic to think he would like the smell of fresh mountain air? I knew I shouldda gone for the odor of malted-milk-ball breath. Just knew it.

My eyes scanned around for something to change the hideously fresh flavor on my tongue to something oatmealy and stale, but there was nothing, nada, zilch.

Of course there wasn't, I thought to myself. We were in a library. So stupid.

Mental note to self: conversation for the rest of the day would have to be limited to only twenty-five letters in the alphabet. No *H* sounds.

"So, like, what's this stupid project on, anyway?" Logan asked.

"Justice," I said.

"I hate justice," Logan responded. "Justice is stupid."

"Too true," I agreed. "Stupid. Matter of fact, I wish I could pound the face of the person who invented justice."

"That would be cool," Logan answered. "Like in a video game."

"Exactly," I answered. "Like in a video game."

Though I really didn't know what I was talking about, Logan seemed to think what I was saying was cool, so that was good enough for me.

I felt around under my chair. Maybe there was a previously chewed piece of bubble gum stuck underneath that I could still suck some juice out of to get rid of the nasty pine taste in my mouth.

I searched. Nope, nothing.

How come a person could never find a good piece of spit-out gum, the kind with all the teeth wrinkles still in it, when they needed it? Life is just so not fair that way.

"Like maybe we could...oh, this is so cool," he began. Logan had a small nose, a dimple in his chin, and messed-up sandy brown hair that looked as if he hadn't combed it since second grade.

So dreamy!

"Like maybe we could do a project on video games," he offered.

"You mean, like connect justice to video games?" I asked, trying to match his enthusiasm. Actually, it wasn't that bad of an idea. I mean, it certainly could be done if we spent some time really thinking about it.

"Naw, forget justice. Justice is stupid," he answered. "Let's just do a project on video games!"

"Mmm, okay," I said. "But, um, Mr. Piddles kind of assigned us a justice project."

"Mr. Piddles is stupid," replied Logan. "And justice is stupid. And stupid school projects about stupid school subjects like stupid justice are stupid. But video games aren't stupid. I mean, even the stupid ones aren't stupid, you know what I mean?"

"Totally," I said. "I totally know what you mean."

Um, what are you talking about? I thought.

"Like, not even the stupid ones are stupid," I added, trying to sound reasonable to him.

"Exactly," he answered.

A pause set in. The awkward kind that's silent and filled with knowing someone should talk but not knowing what to say. I reached under the table. Maybe someone had stuck an old butterscotch under there so I could at least rid my breath of this ridiculous freshness.

Nope. Nada. Nothing. Figures, didn't it?

I scanned the carpet, hoping for something chewable I could scrape up. Chances are it'd be black from people walking on it, but those are the sacrifices of having a crush, right?

"So you got any ideas about this thing, or is this going to be one of those deals where one partner has to do all the work while the other just, like, coasts?" Logan asked. "I mean, no offense, but it seems like I'm the one doing all the deep thinking right now."

"Um, yeah...no...of course," I said. "And now that you ask..." I reached into my backpack. Over the past four nights I had prepared three different project proposals for him to see, each with a different theme.

"So my first idea was that we could do a four quadrant justice diorama where..."

"A diarrhea?" he said.

"A diorama," I answered. "You know, a diorama with like—"

"Diarrhea is funny," he said, laughing. "Like, maybe we

could fart for justice." Logan started making fart sounds. Loud ones under his arm, wet ones by blowing into his elbow. I think he even really farted too, except I didn't hear anything. It was an SBD: Silent But Deadly.

Goodness, did it stink.

Once he was done with his farting display—and this went on for like a good five minutes, with me pretending to be hugely entertained the entire time—I started explaining my idea again. . . .

"So, as I was saying." I pointed to a rough sketch I had done. "We've got the four quadrants of justice and we'll look at how justice is talked about in areas like art, music, books, and movies. I figure we can color code each one in order to—"

"Well, looks like you got a handle on this," Logan said as he stood up.

"You're leaving?" I asked, shocked by the idea of it.

"I'm kinda itchin' to go play some video games," he answered. "I mean, we're all good, right?"

"Um, yeah . . ." I said. "We're all good. I guess. But we'll get together tomorrow again and do some more, right?"

"Is that pine I smell?" he asked, sniffing the air.

I quickly covered my mouth. "Um, no. No. I don't smell anything."

"The woods are stupid," he said.

"Yep, stupid. Totally," I replied.

Logan sniffed again just to be sure. I held in my breath.

"Yeah, tomorrow's coo . . . No wait, can't do tomorrow. I'm already playing video games. But we can do the day after that," he answered.

"Okay," I said. "Same time?"

"Yeah," he replied. "But to be honest, we gotta figure out a way to make these meetings shorter. Not to hurt your feelings or anything, but, well, it kinda felt like, unproductive and disorganized today. I mean, no offense, but my time is sorta valuable."

"I'll, um, try to be more efficient for the next meeting," I told him.

"Would ya? Thanks." Logan pushed his chair under the table. "Later," he said.

"Um, later," I answered.

I watched as he jumped over a chair and zipped out of the library.

I sat there for a moment facing a dilemma. Logan was clearly a wee bit short on the how-sharp-is-my-pencil scale, but he was also hot like a frying pan full of bacon.

Hmm, what was I to do—go for a hot guy with no brains or a brainy guy with no hots?

I thought about it for a moment, but really, it wasn't much of a choice at all. Girls like me, we always know what the right decision is when it comes to stuff like this. We know it deep in our bones.

We want bacon! *Mmmm!*

I blame DNA.

My mind drifted into dreamland. Only two more days til I got to see Logan again. And next time, I'd be prepared.

With milk-ball breath!

inally, after four days of waiting beyond the day we were told we could see the darn thing, Marty put the computer brain into Poochy.

And it didn't work.

Marty had some technological mumbo-jumbo stuff he said was wrong with the dog, but he swore he was going to be able to easily fix it.

And that's what he said the next time and the next time and the next time, too.

For another three days we sat there waiting for this stupid robotic mutt to do something robotic. The most advanced thing it seemed capable of was staring off into the distance with a blank look on its face while wearing a hot pink top that had been sewn by Department Store Mom.

Dumb dog.

"The ThreePees must be quaking in their boots," I said after Marty tried yet again to get the stupid mutt to do what he said it would do.

"Relax, we're close," said Marty. "Very close."

He fiddled with a wire and then programmed a code into his computer for the third time that afternoon.

"Look, let's face reality. We should call this whole thing off before—"

"Look!" said Beanpole.

Suddenly, as if waking from the dead, Poochy sprang to life.

It began with a blink. A moment later Poochy rose to its feet. Actually, it rose to its wheels because it didn't have feet. It gracefully rolled across the floor.

Then, as if it had real eyes that could really see, Poochy came to a stop right in front of Marty.

"Sit," said Marty.

Poochy sat.

"Heel," said Marty.

Poochy walked side by side with Marty as he took a few steps across the garage.

"Speak," said Marty.

"*Aarff*," said Poochy in a voice that sounded exactly like some kind of adorable, fluffy little puppy.

Wow, I thought.

"Roll over!" shouted Beanpole, wanting to try it out herself.

Poochy stopped, processed the instructions, and then, sure enough, rolled over.

"That's amazing!" Beanpole said. "And then, once we

arrange our dance moves, it'll look like this." She rushed across the room, dropped to the ground next to Poochy, and yelled "Roll over!" so she could roll over right next to the dog.

Both Poochy and Beanpole twirled onto their backs at the same time. It looked awesome. However, when Beanpole rolled over, she crashed into the side of a shelf, which caused a box of old cooking pans to fall on her head.

"Ouch!" she said as things collapsed on top of her. "Don't worry, don't worry. I'm okay."

"Try not to kill yourself, Beanpole," I said. "At least until after the talent show, all right?"

"See, I'm using RFID to create programmable animatronics that imitate live action," Marty explained.

"English, please," I said.

Marty rolled his eyes and repeated what he had just told us, but in a language we could understand. "I'm using radio frequency identification tags to basically, well...let's put it this way: you can now program about eighty moves for the dog. I mean, they're already selling stuff like this in the stores but, well...I think it's going to impress people more to see it in a homemade model. Have you mapped out your routine yet?"

"Kind of," I answered. "But we wanted to see how the dog moved first."

Just then Q walked up to the robotic dog, bent down so they were face-to-face, and looked Poochy in the eye.

"Shake," she said.

Poochy raised its paw and extended it out for a shake.

"Play dead," she said.

Poochy laid down and acted as if it were entirely lifeless.

"You say you programmed this stuff based on info you found on the Internet?" asked Q.

"There's tons of stuff out there," said Marty. "But I just put in a few of the basic dog commands. Once you finalize the performance, we'll add in more."

"How long's that gonna take?" asked Q.

"Coupla hours," said Marty. "Not long."

"Poochy, beg," commanded Marty. The robotic dog sat up, bent its front paws, and began to pant and whine and beg as if it were a real dog waiting for some scraps at the dinner table.

"Cool, huh?" he said.

The three of us looked at one another. With matching outfits, a few dance moves, and Poochy, we realized that, holy moly, we weren't gonna be talentless, doof-o-la dipsticks at the talent show after all. Matter of fact, we were gonna rock it.

Rock it like mad!

"This is cool," said Q. "But there's one more part in that bag that I couldn't figure out."

"What?" asked Marty.

"In that black one, over there," she answered. "It looked too big to be part of its head, but I swear, it seems like it needs to be a piece of the dog's ears or something. Can you take a look?"

"Sure," Marty answered, heading over to open the big garbage bag. "No problem."

When he had his back to us, Q eagerly tapped Beanpole and me on the shoulder, trying to get our attention to take a look.

"What?" I said in an annoyed way.

She held her finger to her lips. "Ssshh," she said in a low voice. Then she pointed at Marty. "Look."

I turned to see, though I had no idea in the world what Q was talking about. Marty opened the black bag and *BOOM!* an explosion hit him in the face.

"*Aarrghh!*" he screamed, jumping back. "*Yuucckkk!* What is it?" he exclaimed as giant gobs of white goo dripped from his face and hair.

"Hand lotion," said Q with a smile on her face.

I turned to Q, trying to figure out what had just happened. "You booby-trapped it?"

She took a suck off the scuba tank. *Wheeesh-whooosh. Wheeesh-whooosh.* "Payback time," she said.

Marty struggled to wipe the cream from his eyes. He couldn't even see.

"But I helped you with the dog," he said, still in shock from the explosion.

"That's why I went easy on ya," answered Q. "I was gonna mix in bacon grease, too," she added. "Do you know that when you leave bacon grease and hand lotion mixed together out in the sun for too long, it starts to turn green?" she said. "If I'd have gone all out on you, your head wouldda smelled like rotten meat for three days."

"Gross!" said Beanpole.

"And you can't really wash it out, either," Q added. "So consider yourself lucky."

Marty stared at Q with a face covered in white goop. For a moment, I thought he was going to grab Poochy, shut down his computer, and tell the three of us to go stick the whole talent show up our butts.

But he didn't. Instead, Marty nodded his head and cracked

a smile. "I respect that," he said in this weird, tip-your-hat-to-the-competition type of way. It was as if Q had tapped into some kind of secret code of honor between pranksters or something. "I respect that," he repeated, and then he opened the door to go inside the house and wash everything off.

"What happened to you?" asked my mom, shocked to see her son covered in a face full of goop.

"Nothing," answered Marty, not wanting to admit he'd been pranked. "Now, if you'll excuse me, I gotta go shower. It's all in my ear holes and stuff."

Without another word, Marty headed up the stairs. My mom then peeked her head into the garage, smiling big and bright.

"Good one," she said, giving us a thumbs-up. "Really good one."

Beanpole and I laughed and looked at Q. But Q didn't smile back. Instead she raised the scuba tank and got that Wild West gunfighter look in her eyes again.

"Next up"—*Wheeesh-whooosh. Wheeesh-whooosh*—"the ThreePees."

15

unchtime became giggle time for the three of us. Q and Beanpole and I giggled at the way our math teacher, Mr. Sung-Li, wore four pencils in his shirt pocket in case he was suddenly attacked by a multiplication problem or something. Q and Beanpole and I giggled at the way Josephine Morales tried to hide the fact that she loved the smell of notebook paper. She practically jammed pieces of homework up her nostrils, thinking no one ever saw her. But most of all, Q and Beanpole and I giggled at the dorkasauressness of one another.

"At least I don't crash into parked cars."

"At least I'm not allergic to air."

"At least 254,327 people haven't seen me do a doof-o dance on YouTube."

I paused and got serious. "Is it that many?" Wow, over a quarter of a million people had now seen me utterly embarrass myself.

A quarter million, that's a lot.

"Aw, don't worry," said Q, seeing the gloom on my face. "In like a hundred years, what's it gonna matter anyway?"

"Yeah, I guess you're right."

"Except people will still be able to see you on YouTube in a hundred years," Beanpole said. "'Cause, like, once something's on the Internet, it like never gets erased. Never, ever. But yeah, at least you'll be dead and cold and buried in the ground, so it won't matter much."

"Thanks, Beanpole," I answered. "I can't tell you how much better that makes me feel."

"Even your kids will still be able to see it. And your grand-kids, too. Heck, even your great-great-great-grandkids will be able to see it. I mean, even your great-great-great-great-great... OUCH!"

"Oh, I'm sorry," I said. "Was that your hand underneath the book I just smashed on the table?"

"Don't worry," she said. "I'm okay, I'm okay."

"Who's worried?" I replied.

"Oh no, look who's at it again," said Q. We turned to look at—who else—the ThreePees.

If there was one thing that we loved to giggle about more than making fun of one another's lunches or weird personalities or dorkiness, it was the ThreePees. At the way they sprayed all that stuff in their hair. At the way they wore their name-brand clothing as if designer labels made them better people than every-body else. The way they walked with an extra wiggle in their butts. Lately, however, we'd been having extra fun giggling at the way Sofes O'Reilly, the Albert Einstein of our school, still kept screwing up that make-a-right-not-a-left turn at the crucial part of their dance performance.

"It's a right turn, Sofes. A right turn!" said Kiki for the ten-thousandth time. Clearly, Sofes was driving Kiki bonkers.

"I know, I know," said Sofes. "I just get mixed up there. It feels more natural to go left."

"It's gonna feel more natural to go to a different school next year if you don't get your act together," snapped Kiki. "The show is in three days!"

"The show is in three days!" said Q in a high-pitched snooty voice. "And if I don't win and get my picture in the yearbook, I'll never be named the Queen of the Universe like my daddy promised when he paid all that money for my fake eyelashes."

The three of us laughed. Loud. A bit too loud, I think, because Kiki seemed to know we were laughing at her.

She stormed over to our table.

"What's so funny?" she demanded. The rest of the ThreePees followed behind her like good little donkeys.

"Nothing," said Q, looking at the ground, trying to hide her smile.

"Well, something's gotta be funny if it's making the school's biggest dorkwads laugh," said Kiki.

None of us answered. We just looked at one another and continued to try and hide our giggles.

"So what's your talent anyway, doof cheese?" Kiki asked in a biting tone.

"Nothing," answered Beanpole. "We don't have any talent."

"You got that right," said Brittany-Brattany.

"I mean, we're not telling," replied Beanpole. "It's super

secret. Like top secret. Like you could torture us right now and light our fingernails on fire and put us in a pit of poison scorpions and we'd never tell. Never, ever, ever!"

"You mean you'd never tell me about the robotic dog?" said Kiki.

Beanpole's jaw dropped to the floor.

"I know all about your lame metal mutt," said Kiki. "Logan told me everything."

Beanpole and Q turned to me. I looked at my shoes.

Oops.

"But you last-place finishers in life really don't think you have a chance with this stupid dog idea, do you?" said Kiki.

"Yeah, do you?" added Sofes.

"The question is," said Q, pausing to take a scuba slurp before finishing her sentence—*Wheeesh-whooosh. Wheeesh-whooosh*—"do you?"

"Do we what?" said Kiki. "What are you talking about, dodo breath?"

"Yeah," repeated Sofes. "What are you talking about, dodo breath?"

"I'm talking about the fact that we're makin' you nervous, aren't we, Kiki?" said Q.

"Who's making me nervous, allergy freak?"

Wheeesh-whooosh. Wheeesh-whooosh. "We are. We're making you sweat."

"Are not."

"Are too."

"Are not."

"Are too."

"Are not, ya loser."

"Are too! Are too! Are too!"

"Well, if we're not making you nervous," I said, rising to stand next to Q, "then why are you over here right now asking us all of these questions, Keeks?"

I said that last part, the word *Keeks*, with a whole lotta *oomph.*

Silence fell over the ThreePees as they thought about what I had just said. I could tell they realized I was right. They were nervous. They were feeling afraid. For the first time ever, the idea that they might not actually win the talent show had entered their minds, and it rattled 'em.

Rattled 'em good.

Suddenly, sensing blood in the water, Q got that Wild West gunfighter look in her eyes again.

"You witches best get ready"—*Wheeesh-whooosh. Wheeesh-whooosh*—"'cause it's payback time."

"Yeah," said Beanpole, standing up as well. "It's payback time."

Beanpole got face-to-face with Sofes. Q glared at Brittany-Brattany. Seeing what they were doing, I quickly took a step forward and got right up into Kiki's grille.

"That's what the Nerd Girls are talking 'bout, Keeks," I said. "Payback time!"

The six of us stood there nose to nose, three on one side, three one the other, having a monster stare down.

A moment later, amazingly, the ThreePees backed off.

"Come on, girls," said Kiki, turning to walk away. "In

seventy-two hours, we'll see who's got the tears and who's got the trophy."

"Yeah," said Brittany-Brattany as she flipped her hair and turned to walk away as well.

"Yeah," said Sofes. "Just wait and we'll see how you like having the trophy."

"The tears, Sofes...they're going to have the tears," said Kiki with a shake of her head. "*We're* going to have the trophy."

"Oh," said Sofes as they wiggled away. "See, I thought it was like a tears of joy type of thing and they'd be carrying the trophy of sadness, know what I mean?"

"No, I don't know what you mean, Sofes. Half the time I have no idea what you mean," snapped Kiki. "So how about if you just focus on learning your right from your left and leave the rest of the thinking to me, okay, you mental midget?"

"Like, harsh again," said Sofes.

"Like, true again," replied Kiki.

"You've heard of the trophy of sadness, right Brit?" said Sofes, seeking a bit of compassion from her other donkey friend.

"Let's just make sure we win, okay?" answered Brattany. "Like my dad always says, the only thing that matters in this world is when you win."

The ThreePees returned to their spot on the other side of the courtyard and got ready to practice their routine again.

"We did it!" said Beanpole. "Didya see? They're scared! They're scared!"

"I saw that they knew all about Poochy," said Q with a look toward me.

"Sorry," I said. "Blame DNA."

"Uh-huh," said Q.

"Well, I told you I was no good at keeping secrets," I added. "You can't trust me with hush-hush stuff at all. I mean, I spoil surprise parties and everything."

"It's okay," said Q. "Crushes'll make you do weird things."

"Ain't that the truth," I said. "I can't believe how much work I am doing on this stupid justice project right now. Logan is just a total flake."

Beanpole stared at the ThreePees as they worked on their moves.

"You know, there's nothing they can do to stop us now anyway," she said in her life-is-never-perky-enough type of way. And then she turned to Q and me. "We are on fire!"

And we were on fire, too. That afternoon the three of us met at Beanpole's house to finalize the performance with Poochy, and it went great.

Just great.

"And three, two, one..." I called out. The four of us—me and Beanpole and Q and Poochy—marched in a straight line, then Poochy broke off and we formed a semicircle. I wasn't a good dancer, but we kept all the moves simple so we were synched up with the dog in a way that was fun and fresh. Plus, we knew we'd all be dressed the same, so that would make us look even more professional.

As we marched in place to the beat, Beanpole pulled out a plastic fire hydrant that Department Store Mom had made, and she put it in the center of our semicircle. Then, as we stomped our feet and lifted our knees in 4/4 time, Poochy rolled into the center of the circle, lifted its doggie leg, and took a pee.

That's right, our grand finale was for Poochy to take a giant pee, center stage, in front of the whole audience!

Department Store Mom had even put yellow food coloring in the dog's water tank to make it look like real doggie whiz.

It was SO funny that we laughed every time we got to that last part of our performance. I couldn't believe Marty was able to program such a cool move into the robot's system. We tried it six times, and each time it worked perfectly.

"Hey, I have an idea," said Beanpole after we'd finished another round. "How about if we put lemonade in the tank, and then after Poochy pees, we'll all drink a glass."

"And why would we do that?" I asked.

"'Cause it would be funny," she answered.

"You think drinking pee is funny?" I said.

"I do," she answered.

"Then why don't we just put brownies in its butt and eat dog poop, too?"

"Eating dog poop's not funny, Mo," answered Beanpole. "Not funny at all."

"But drinking dog pee is?" I said.

"There's a difference."

"Oh yeah, what?"

"I don't know," she said. "But there is."

"Whadda you think, Q?" I asked. "Is eating dog poop more or less funny than drinking dog pee?"

"I'm allergic to animal urine. Makes my thumbs throb."

"You know, have you ever thought about calling the *Guinness Book*?" I asked. "Really, you might be missing out on a great opportunity here so get some good attention for your weirdness."

"I'll put it on my to-do list," she answered. "Right next to eating brownies out of a doggie's butt."

"She's right," said Beanpole, taking Q's side of the argument. "I can't believe you want to put brownies in the dog's butt and eat them," she said. "That's gross."

"You're right, Beanpole, it is gross," I said. "And the next time my neighbor's cat takes a pee, I'll make sure to pour you a glass of kitty-squirt to cool you off on a hot summer's day, 'cause that's not gross at all."

"Ew!" said Beanpole.

"Can we just get back to practicing?" said Q.

"You're right," I said. "Okay, let's take it from the top."

We took our positions.

The music started. Then I pushed the STOP button.

"I need a break," I said, stepping out of formation.

"Not again, Maureen," whined Beanpole as I headed toward the door.

"Well, all this talk about pee makes me have to go again," I said.

"But you just went."

"You brought it up, not me," I answered.

"You're still hydrating?" asked Q.

"Uh-huh," I answered. "But what I don't get is why, when I am only putting in a quart a day, two quarts seem to come out."

After my bathroom break, we practiced and practiced and practiced, and though the whole routine was only going to be

124

about three minutes long, each time we did it, we got better and better and better. Plus, Department Store Mom had added sparkles to the outfits, Marty had synced the beat of the sound track to the steps of the dog, and even though Q couldn't really move too fast or do any kind of crazy flips or anything, 'cause she'd quickly lose her breath—not that I could either—the small steps that we were able to choreograph had evolved into something that looked really sweet.

Poochy was the star of the show, we were the sidekicks, and yet as a group, we made for one heck of a team.

"I gotta go," I said after the last run-through.

"Aw, just fifteen more minutes," said Beanpole.

"That's what you said fifteen minutes ago," I answered. "Really, I gotta go finish this justice project. It's due tomorrow, and Piddles will piddle in his pants if we don't do a good job."

"How come he didn't give our class a justice project?" Q asked Beanpole. They had Piddles for fifth period while I had him for second.

"He said that Mo's class talks too much so they needed the extra work," Beanpole answered. "Said it was justice for them."

"Good for us," said Q. "And stinks for you."

"Don't I know it," I said, gathering up my stuff.

"Sure, just go back to your *smoochy-smoochy* boyfriend and leave us here hangin'," said Q.

"He's not my *smoochy-smoochy* boyfriend," I responded. "And I am not leaving you hangin'. We just practiced for like a hundred hours."

"Is Logan coming to your house, or are you going to his?" asked Beanpole.

"Yeah, where's all the *smoochy-smooching* going to take place?" asked Q after a *wheeesh-whooosh*.

"There's not going to be any *smoochy-smooching*," I said and then I made a *Wheeesh-whooosh, Wheeesh-whooosh* sound to tease Q back like she was teasing me. "Especially since I'm pretty much doing the whole project by myself."

"He really hasn't helped you, huh?" asked Beanpole.

"Only to tell me when he thinks something is stupid," I said. "And Logan seems to think a lot of things are stupid. He thinks staplers are stupid, hamburger buns without seeds are stupid, and stupid justice projects for stupid teachers in stupid schools are stupid. Like they are even more stupid than stupid video games, and, as we all know, even stupid video games aren't really all that stupid. Not like stupid justice projects, at least."

"What are you talking about?" asked Beanpole.

"Forget it. It's complicated," I answered. "See you guys later; I gotta go."

"Mo, wait, before you leave…"

I stopped.

"Yeah?"

Suddenly, Q got all shy and timid.

"I was…" She drifted off.

"Yeah, Q?"

"I was…" She paused again, for like, a really long time.

"What, Q?" I snapped. "Spit it out, ya freakwad. I told you, I gotta go."

"I was…" She took another suck off the scuba tank. *Wheeesh-whooosh. Wheeesh-whooosh.* "I was thinking my mom could drive us to the talent show. You know, like you guys could maybe come over to my house and we could all ride over together or something?"

Beanpole looked up.

"Come to your house?" I said.

Q's eyes immediately dropped to the floor, as if she was expecting instant rejection.

Beanpole, in her perky way, started smiling and shaking her head up and down, like someone had just plugged her brain into an electrical outlet with really high voltage. She mouthed the words *Say yes—and be nice.*

"I am nice, you stick figure ding-dong!" I yelled at her. Q gazed up with a nervous look on her face. "Sorry, wasn't talking to you," I said.

"I mean, the thing is, I haven't told you guys," said Q, lowering her eyes again, preparing to let us in on yet another one of her million personal secrets. "Is . . . well, I get really nervous around crowds. Like, the idea of being onstage in front of a whole buncha people freaks me out. It's why I never talk in class even when I know the answer."

She paused. Neither Beanpole nor I said anything.

"Like, it really freaks me out, I'm serious. More than you know, and I, well . . . I'm scared I am not going to be able to make it and might start hyperventilating and have a panic attack and have to go for a walk or something."

She shuffled her feet.

"A long walk. A long, long, long walk. Walking's the only thing that calms me down."

The three of us were quiet for a minute.

"Aw, don't sweat it, Q," I finally said. "We're gonna be there too, ya weirdo."

"Yeah," added Beanpole. "We'll be right there with you the whole time. And of course we'll drive over together. It'll be fun to come to your house and see where you live."

"I just...I get nervous, that's all. Almost like I can't control it," she added. "The panic attacks I get, well...I'm just scared I'm gonna flip out. Is that bad?"

"Bad?" I said. "Heck no. I mean, I get stage fright too. Matter of fact, I'm scared I might pee onstage before Poochy does."

We all laughed.

"They can just add it to your YouTube clip," said Beanpole with a smile.

"Oh great, just what I need," I said. "Naw, don't sweat it, Q." I picked up my backpack. "We'll meet at your house and ride together. It'll be cool."

"Yeah," said Beanpole. "We'll turn your mom's car into the Nerd Mobile."

We laughed again.

"And with a little luck," added Beanpole, "we can make it all the way there without having to stop so Mo can take a wee."

"Speaking of wee," I said.

"Not again, Mo."

"What?" I said in my own defense. "I can't help it."

After yet another trip to the Department Store Bathroom, where the toilet paper was always folded with a little triangle on the end of the roll, as if I were in a fancy hotel or something, I went back into the bedroom to get my backpack.

"See you tomorrow," I said, heading for the door.

"See ya, Mo," they answered. "And good luck with the project."

"Yeah, good luck is right," I answered. "I'm sure I'll be up until midnight."

"I wonder how many pees that is?" said Beanpole to Q. They laughed.

I stopped, turned, and put down my backpack.

"You had to say something, didn't you, Beanpole? You just had to say something."

During second period the next day, Mr. Piddles walked to the left, walked to the right, looked up, looked down, and inspected our justice project from almost every possible angle he could.

"A diorama, huh?" he said.

There was a pause. I guess it was up to me to explain.

"Yes, sir," I began. "With each of the four quadrants representing justice in famous works of art, music, literature, and cinema."

"Cinema?" he said.

"Yeah, you know, the movies," I answered. "I mean, movies can be art too, right?"

"Hmmm," he answered as he took it all in. "Well thought out. Very well thought out."

"Thank you, sir."

Logan sat there feeling good about things.

"And I am sure you contributed, um, to this project, did you not, Mr. Meyers?"

"Um, well...yeah," Logan said. "Um, of the diarrhea-a-ma thing, yeah, it's fifty percent mine."

"And which fifty percent would that be?" Mr. Piddles asked Logan.

"Well, um...the fifty percent where, um..." He started to stumble. Truth is, Logan hadn't even looked at the whole project entirely. I doubt he even knew half of the stuff I had put in there.

"Like, well, my fifty percent comes from the stupid stuff," Logan explained, trying to sound intelligent. "Like the stupid stuff you don't see. Like the woods and the hamburger buns without seeds and some video games, like the stuff that's not there 'cause it's stupid. I helped to do and to not do that," he replied.

The forehead of Mr. Piddles crinkled. I could tell he was thinking *Huh?*

Mr. Piddles turned to me.

"Did your partner contribute fifty percent of this work, Miss Saunders?" he asked me in a direct tone. "Because when partners do not contribute, it's not what I call *just*."

He stared at Logan with a deep, menacing look in his eye.

"And you know how I feel about justice, do you not, Mr. Meyers?"

Mr. Piddles continued to stare. Logan slouched in his seat.

After all my effort, all my hard work, all the meetings that Logan had blown off, all the lack of contribution from him top to bottom, well...the truth is, I was finally glad that someone was about to make Logan pay for it. I mean, it just wasn't fair what he had put me through. I had done everything. Everything!

And he had done nothing, yet now he was about to get half the credit for this big project, when he didn't really deserve squat.

It wasn't . . . It wasn't *just.*

And so what if he was cute, I thought. Pulling junk like that on people is not cool no matter who you are. I mean, why do all the good-looking people always feel they are entitled to take advantage of us regular folks anyway? It's not right.

It's not fair.

I was mad, madder than I even realized, and suddenly I felt like expressing it. Not just expressing it, but exploding!

"You know, Mr. Piddles, I should take full credit," I forcefully began.

Logan's eyes got as big as baseballs.

"And I want to take credit, too," I continued.

Mr. Piddles glared at Logan. Logan slinked even further into his seat. He knew he was looking at after-school detention all the way till he graduated from college, or something crazy like that.

"But to take credit when credit is not yours would not be *just*, now, would it?" I added. "And if there is one thing this project taught me, it's about how people need to be just to one another. Otherwise, society cannot function, right? So yes, Logan did fifty percent of the work. He deserves his points as much as I do."

Logan, totally surprised by my answer, gazed around with a what-the-heck-is-going-on look on his face, then sat up straight in his chair. A bit of pride even flashed in his eyes, and suddenly his expression changed from a look of *Oh my goodness I am toast*, to *Yeah, I do deserve some academic credit—how could you even doubt me?*

"Whatever grade I get is the grade that Logan should get," I added. "It's only right. We're partners, fifty-fifty all the way."

"Fifty-fifty?" asked Mr. Piddles for clarification.

"Fifty-fifty," I replied. Even if Mr. Piddles knew the truth, I wasn't going to snitch on Logan. Karma would get him one day. Not me. That's just not how I roll.

Mr. Piddles looked down at his grading sheet, made a few notes, and softly said, "Very well." Then, he walked away to grade another student's work.

Once he was gone, Logan stared at me. But he didn't just look; he kinda gazed.

"That was cool," he said.

"Uh-huh," I said, putting some stuff away in my backpack. The bell was getting ready to ring. Logan continued to gawk at me.

He had some of the deepest blue eyes I had ever seen.

"Like, you're pretty cool, you know that?" he continued. "Like pretty, totally cool."

"Thanks," I said, zipping up the outside pocket of my backpack.

"And not stupid either," he added. "I mean, not stupid like some other people are stupid, know what I mean?"

I guess that was some kind of compliment.

"Yeah, um, thanks," I answered.

I looked up and turned to face him. We were less than four inches apart. He stared at me in a way that made it feel as if a dream spell were being sent my way. I thought my heart was going to melt.

But it didn't. My heart didn't melt at all. Matter of fact, it just continued to beat the way it always did, one *tha-dump* at a time.

There was no magic, no sparkle, no wild elks running in the distance. Now that Logan and I were face-to-face in the middle of class after having finished our justice project, I suddenly realized, *This dude is kind of a dud*.

"Hey, you wanna, you know, like maybe go hang out or something at the mall sometime?" he asked.

The bell rang.

"Uh, thanks, but I'm kinda busy these days. You know, the talent show and all," I said, picking up my stuff. "Maybe another time."

I stood, placed the diorama on the counter where Mr. Piddles had asked us all to leave our projects, and left.

Just left.

Was I bonkers? Was I really turning down a date at the mall with Logan Meyers, the Greek god of middle school boys?

Yep, sure was.

I walked out of class thinking, *I need to get my head examined*, when suddenly my two doof-o-la partners ran up to me in the hall, looking like they had the worst possible news ever in the world to give me. They were panicked.

"What's wrong?" I asked. They didn't even want to know how things had gone with Logan.

"They're making us do a dress rehearsal," said Beanpole.

"What?" I replied.

"A"—*Wheeesh-whooosh. Wheeesh-whooosh*—"dress rehearsal," repeated Q.

"Why?"

Q's cheeks started turning red. "'Cause last year it was"—*Wheeesh-whooosh. Wheeesh-whooosh*—"too chaotic with all the acts not knowing"—*Wheeesh-whooosh. Wheeesh-whooosh*—"who went when and in what order, and"—*Wheeesh-whooosh. Wheeesh-whooosh*—"what was supposed to be an hour-and-a-half show took three and a half hours, so they"—*Wheeesh-whooosh. Wheeesh-whooosh*—"are making all competitors do a dress rehearsal so that they can"—*Wheeesh-whooosh. Wheeesh-whooosh*—"be practiced and speed things up 'cause they"—*Wheeesh-whooosh. Wheeesh-whooosh*—"don't want kids out till"—*Wheeesh-whooosh. Wheeesh-whooosh*—"eleven thirty p.m."

I stared in amazement. "That might be the weirdest explanation I've ever seen."

"She's nervous," said Beanpole.

"No kidding," I answered. "So when are they having this little dress rehearsal?" I asked.

"Today," said Beanpole.

"Today?" I replied.

"After school," said Beanpole.

"After school?" I repeated.

"At four fifteen," said Beanpole.

"At four fifteen?!" I exclaimed.

I paused and tried to figure it all out.

"Holy moly, gimme a slurp of that," I said, grabbing Q's scuba tank. I tried to do a *Wheeesh-whooosh. Wheeesh-whooosh* of my own but couldn't figure out how to operate the dumb thing. Suddenly I looked up and realized that both Beanpole and Q were staring at me in horror.

Genuine horror.

Beanpole looked about as white as a mayonnaise sandwich, and Q looked like she was about to go into super-hyperventilate mode at any second. Like it or not, I had become the unofficial leader of this group of dorkasauruses, and they were counting on me to do something or say something or realize something that would let them know that everything was going to be okay.

What they wanted me to do, I had no idea, but I did realize that I had to come up with something, and something quick, or one of them might go into nerdiac arrest.

I straightened my spine, raised my chin, and proudly puffed out my chest. They waited eagerly.

"I have to pee," I said, and raced to the bathroom, abandoning them in the hallway.

A dress rehearsal? I thought. We're toast!

After I took two pees—'cause the news of this mandatory dress rehearsal was way too big of a nuclear bomb to just take one—we made plans to meet by the Fountain before the dress rehearsal began to get our act together.

The Fountain at Grover Park Middle School was like this really important traditional thing in front of the performing arts center. Basically, it was this big Italian-style fountain with this half-naked guy in it who spit water out of his mouth. It was built something like sixty years ago, when the school first opened, and each year the tradition was for the graduating eighth graders to jump in and take a swim once they had earned their certificates of graduation. However, the Fountain was only like two feet deep, so a person couldn't really swim in it; they could just sort of get totally wet, but whatever, it was tradition, right?

Anyway, that was our plan, to meet by the Fountain at 4:05 and re-gather ourselves. After all, we were already nervous about performing on Saturday night, and now they wanted us to perform on Friday afternoon, too, just to make sure that the show went smoothly? It was enough to make Q buy a second scuba tank.

I rushed home, explained to Marty about the dress rehearsal, and picked up Poochy.

"She's all ready to go," he said, handing me the mutt. "Tip-top shape."

"Like really ready?" I asked.

"Like really ready."

"Like totally ready?" I said.

"Like totally ready."

"Like one hundred percent, nothing will go wrong, more ready than any other robotic dog that has ever heeled or barked or played dead on the face of this planet ready?" I said. My heart was beating a hundred miles an hour.

"Relax, you dweeb," Marty said. "Poochy is ready, and if you don't get a grip on yourself, it's you who is going to screw things up, not him."

I let out a sigh.

"It's okay to be nervous, Boo," said my mom. "But the key is not to let the fear kill all the fun and excitement. Go enjoy yourselves, have a good time, and things will work out great."

"They will?" I said, wanting to believe her.

"They will," she replied. "Remember, if you think positive, positive things happen."

There she went again, more mumbo-jumbo stuff. I just hoped she was right.

I put Poochy in my backpack, took three deep breaths, and

went to my room to get changed. Five minutes later I dashed out the front door wearing the pink-and-black outfit Department Store Mom had made for us.

"Bye," I said.

"Good luck, Boo," answered my mom.

"We'll need it," I replied.

"You look cute," said Ashley. I stopped and stared at her. She wasn't being sarcastic.

"Really," she said. "You do. And I'm going to bring the whole gymnastic team tomorrow night to support you."

"Your whole team."

"The whole team," she said. "They're really strong and can cheer really loud."

I shook my head. I didn't have time to deal with normalcy from my sister. It was way too bonkers.

"Well," I said, "ready or not, here we come," and I closed the door behind me.

I was off to school.

When I finally got to the Fountain, my Nerd Girl partners were waiting for me. Q was sucking on the scuba tank more than she was breathing regular air, and Beanpole had grown so pale she looked like a zombie from Planet String Bean. They were in terrible shape.

Then I realized something. Ashley was right; I did look good. I mean, I hadn't made a stop at the Paradise Palace in quite some time, and to tell the truth, I didn't miss it at all.

Not at all.

I looked more closely at Beanpole and Q. Heck, it wasn't just me who looked good; we all looked good. We Nerd Girls looked totally sharp in our custom-made outfits. For some reason, it was a thought that calmed me down.

"How ya feelin'?" I asked as I walked up.

"Nervous. Freaking out. Scared I am going to die without ever having had the chance to drive a car, French kiss a boy, or ride an elephant backward in Thailand."

"Ride an elephant backward in Thailand?" I said.

"Hey, we all have dreams, right?" Beanpole answered. "Besides, I haven't walked into any walls or bumped my head once this afternoon, so something is definitely wrong with me. I mean, I never go more than a few hours without some sort of painful injury."

"And you, Q?" I asked. "How you doin'?"

"I'm kinda feeling like I might need to go for a walk," she answered. "To Hawaii."

I smiled. "Your mom did a nice job with the tank tops," I said to Beanpole. "I mean, I can't see Q's scar at all."

I pointed to where the black tank top covered Q's craggy wound.

"You can't?" said Q, a bit self-conscious that I had even mentioned her old injury.

"Nope," I answered. "And the colors look good on you, Beanpole. They make that shade of white you are turning look really hot."

She laughed.

"Face it..." I said. "We look kind of fresh."

We took a moment to gaze at one another, to check out the way we were dressed. Soon, Beanpole and Q realized I was right.

We did look fresh. I could see the tension starting to melt off their faces.

"Did you bring Poochy?" asked Beanpole, showing signs of life.

"Of course," I answered. "Got him right here."

I pulled out the dog and set him on the ground. It was amazing how his outfit matched ours so perfectly. Department Store Mom had really nailed it.

"And he works?" asked Q in a steadier voice.

"Works perfect," I answered. "Marty says we're all set."

I could tell they wanted to believe me, but still sorta didn't.

"You know, it's okay to be scared," I said. "But we don't want the fear to kill all the fun, do we?"

Oh my goodness, who was I, my mom? However, they both looked at me like I was making sense, so I continued.

"Let's just go have a good time, huh?" I said. "After all, when you think positive, positive things happen."

Now I was really turning into my mom. Scary.

"Besides, we've practiced this a hundred times," I reasoned.

Had motherly aliens taken over my body? HELP!

"Two hundred," said Beanpole.

Goodness, it was working.

"And just think about how great it's going to be to squash the ThreePees like a package of chocolate pudding," I added.

Now, that sounded more like me. Q took a suck off the scuba tank.

"Yeah,"—*Wheeesh-whooosh. Wheeesh-whooosh*—"crush 'em like a pack of chocolate pudding."

Then I saw it, the thing I was hoping for, the look of the Wild West gunfighter in Q's eyes.

"Let's go get them witches," she said. *Wheeesh-whooosh. Wheeesh-whooosh.* "Let's go get 'em good."

"Look, we know our steps, we look hot, and Poochy is ready to rock," I said. "I mean, we are about as ready as we're ever going to be, right?"

"Right!" they said.

"Come on, Nerd Girls," I said, picking up Poochy and heading into the auditorium. "It's SHOWTIME!"

And with that I led my friends into the auditorium. It was a glorious moment filled with energy, excitement, and enthusiasm.

Unfortunately, it was a moment that only lasted about eleven seconds, because as soon as we got backstage, we wished we could go hide under a rock.

"Ha-ha, nice outfits, doof-o-ramas."

We turned when we heard Kiki's voice. The realization hit us at the same time.

The ThreePees were still dressed in their regular school clothes. *Huh?*

"I guess you dork-balls didn't realize that dress rehearsal doesn't mean you actually have to dress," said Kiki with a cackle.

We looked around. No one was else dressed in their special clothes for tomorrow night's show either. Not Puking Patty. Not Johnny the Jerk-O Jaspers. Not even Loser Lloyd Weinersnorter, the kid with the worst last name in school history. We were the only ones.

"But you look *soooo* cute," said Brittany-Brattany with a sarcastic bite. "Just *ah-door-ah-billl*!"

"Yeah," said Sofes. "*Ah-door-ah-billl*!"

Click! Brattany took our picture to document our stupidness.

The ThreePees enjoyed a huge laugh and then they encouraged some other kids to laugh at us too.

"Nice sparkles," said Puking Patty. "Did your mommy make those for you?"

"Yeah, did your mommy make those for you?" added Weinersnorter. With a kid named Weinersnorter ridiculing us, we knew we had sunk to a pretty low level. Me and Beanpole and Q had just become the center of attention for exactly the wrong reason, and everyone was staring at us.

Everyone.

"What a buncha dinkus heads," laughed Kiki.

"Yeah, dinkus heads," said Sofes. "With extra mustard on top."

I felt like we were wearing tuxedoes in a restaurant where all the other people were wearing shorts and T-shirts. It was uncomfortable. Very uncomfortable. In the blink of an eye we had gone from feeling really good and confident and positive about ourselves to feeling awkward and dorky and doofy all over again. Our confidence had vanished.

"Everybody, please make sure to check the sheet to see the order in which you will be appearing," announced Mr. Piddles, the lead judge of the show. "And be sure to be ready when it's your turn to come onstage."

At least that was a sliver of good news. Though I am not sure how she did it, Q's connection in the nurse's office had done us a favor and rigged the appearance order for talent show so that we, the Nerd Girls, would get to perform last. That meant we were going to be the grand finale, and as everyone knows, if you really want to win a talent show, the best place to appear is last, because if you do a really great job, the judges will remember it the most and you have the best chance of winning.

But Q and Beanpole didn't find all that much comfort in seeing that we were going to be last. They were still flipping out about our being the only ones in performance clothes.

"I mean, no one told us that dress rehearsal didn't mean we had to dress," said Beanpole, completely puzzled by the whole thing. "I just assumed that . . ."

Q started to hyperventilate. Kiki came over to try and make our lives even more miserable.

"By the way," she said, turning her attention directly toward Q, "I hope your little mechanical mutt doesn't get stage fright. I mean, you do know there's going to be A LOT of people watching tomorrow night."

"Yeah, a whole lot," said Brittany-Brattany, speaking almost directly to Q.

"Like, even more than a whole lot," added Sofes. "I whole lotta lot."

The ThreePees were playing head games with us—especially with Q. I think they knew, based on how shy she was about speaking up in class, that stage fright was something that might really get to her.

Especially if they got her to spend the next twenty-four hours thinking about it. Anxiety is one of those things that always builds upon itself.

It was a mean, nasty, low-down strategy. But worst of all—as I could see by the color of green Q was turning—it was working.

"Good luck out there, Nerd Girls," said Kiki, turning away now that her mission was accomplished. "And remember, only about a thousand people will be watching you tomorrow night."

"Yeah, a thousand people," said Brattany.

"That's two thousand eyeballs," said Kiki.

"Yeah, two thousand eyeballs," said Brattany.

"And four thousand nostrils," added Sofes.

Everyone stopped and turned. Sofes paused.

"I mean two thousand nostrils," she said. "Wait, how many eyeballs is it?"

Kiki didn't even bother to answer.

"Just remember, whatever you do, don't panic, allergy girl," said Kiki. "I mean, it's not like anybody is going to be filming this or anything."

Just then Brittany-Brattany reached into her purse and flashed her video camera.

"Can you say YouTube, disease freak?" added Kiki. The three of them screeched like happy little witches as they walked away.

"What do nostrils have to do with watching anybody, Sofes?" asked Brittany-Brattany.

"I was just trying to scare them," Sofes said. "I mean, lots of people are afraid of nostrils 'cause, like, that's where boogers hide."

I swear the girl was hopeless.

The ThreePees drifted over to the other side of the auditorium, their work done.

"I need to go for a walk," said Q.

"You don't need to go for a walk," I answered.

"No, I need to go for a walk," she said. "Now."

"Listen to me, Q," I insisted, grabbing her arm and stopping her. "You don't need to go for a walk. Now is the time to be strong. To be brave. To not give in to these jerks. All my life they have tortured me, and ever since you came to this school, they have tortured you too. Now's the time to stand up to them, to put them in their place, to make them lick our boots. Can you do that for me, Q? Can you be strong for just three minutes?"

Q raised her eyes.

"Just three minutes? That's all I am asking."

She looked at me with sad, puppy dog eyes. Slowly, she turned to look at Beanpole. There wasn't a shred of strength to be found in Q. Quietly, thoughtfully, she lifted the scuba tank and took a deep, slow slurp.

Wheeesh-whooosh. Wheeesh-whooosh.

"I can," she said. "I can."

A flash of strength crossed through her eyes, and Beanpole smiled. I smiled too. However, Q didn't smile. She didn't show any teeth at all. Instead she just gazed off into the distance like a Wild West gunfighter getting ready for her big shoot-out.

"Places, everyone," announced Mr. Piddles. "Take your places, please."

Ready or not, here we come.

I can't even begin to describe all the loser performances we had to sit through before it was our turn. People singing off-key, people juggling and dropping plates, people playing musical instruments in a way that made me want to smash their flutes. We must have been the most talentless middle school in the United States of America.

"I swear," I said to Q and Beanpole after watching some goober try to turn Shakespeare into hip-hop but forgetting, like, every other line, "if they gave awards for this stuff, our school would come in first place in the category of Most Moronic Putz-o-ramas Ever Assembled In One Building. I mean, why is Pepperoni Paulie trying to ride a unicycle when he is so fat he needs to turn sideways to enter a classroom? Really, how hard was it to figure out that he was going to crash?"

"It's like we always thought," said Q. "There's only one group that's going to present any real competition."

"And here they come," said Beanpole. "Here they come."

Finally, after all those losers, it was the ThreePees's turn. They'd been scheduled to go right before us. Kiki, Brattany, and Sofes took the stage, and suddenly it was like the whole mood in the auditorium changed, even though the performing arts center was pretty much empty aside from a few teachers sitting in the front row. No, they didn't have their fireworks set up yet, and no, they didn't have their balloons yet. They didn't even have their dance uniforms on, but still, once the ThreePees stood center stage and got ready to do their thing, there was no doubt about it—they had an energy that was electric.

And their routine was smoking! Great music, excellent dance moves, just a ton of awesomeness. Beanpole and Q and I watched from the sidelines in awe. There was no doubt that, as much as we had practiced, as much as we had tried, as much as we had made up a fun show with a cute little robotic dog, the ThreePees were like some sort of professional force of nature. Clearly, we were amateurs next to them, and the longer they performed, the more I realized how much better they were.

We had no chance. No chance at all to beat them. At least that's what I thought, until...

Until Sofes O'Reilly messed up the turn.

Yep, Sofes screwed up the turn. She went left when she was supposed to go right, and since the move that followed was some kind of synchronized jump that ended in a split, their whole routine was thrown off.

Worse, however, was that Sofes had stopped dancing after she'd messed up, while Kiki had kept going and Brittany-Brattany sort of half danced and half waited to see what they were going to do next.

Confusion took over. The ThreePees, suddenly lost and disorganized, had gone in a split-second's time from NFL cheerleaders to out-of-sync middle school kids totally unsure of which way to go, how to proceed, or what to do next. They bumbled to a stop.

"It's okay, girls," said Mr. Piddles. "I'm sure you'll get it right tomorrow."

"No, let's do it again," said Kiki, taking her starting position.

"There's no need, Miss Masters," replied Mr. Piddles. "This rehearsal is just for timing. Tomorrow night's the real deal. Next group, please," he called out.

"But I want to do it again," said Kiki in a forceful voice. "So we get it right." Deep rage flashed in her eyes. "Come on, line up!" she ordered. "Let's take it from the top."

"I said there was no need," said Mr. Piddles. "Your group will go tomorrow."

"But we need to do it again. Right now!" answered Kiki, defying the teacher. "Now, I said 'Line up,'" she said to Sofes and Brittany-Brattany.

The two girls stared.

"No, do not line up," replied Mr. Piddles in a sharp tone. "It's getting late, we all want to get home, and there's only one more group to go, so please leave the stage. As I said, you'll have your chance tomorrow."

Brittany-Brattany and Sofes stood there like two lost little donkeys waiting for Kiki to let them know what to do. But Kiki didn't budge. The tension grew.

"I said," Mr. Piddles added, "please leave the—"

"But Mr. Piddles, you don't understand," interrupted Kiki. "We need to get this right in order to—"

"No, Miss Masters, you don't understand," interrupted Mr. Piddles. "I am asking you to please leave the stage before I take serious action."

Kiki didn't move. "Mr. Piddles, you don't seem to get that in order for us to—"

"Action such as disqualification," said Mr. Piddles, rising from his seat.

Kiki stayed put. The top of Mr. Piddles's bald head started to turn red. However, Kiki still stood there defiantly. A terrified look came over the faces of Sofes and Brittany-Brattany. Everyone in the theater froze. Kiki looked like she was about to have a major-league temper tantrum, some kind of full-blown meltdown aimed directly at Mr. Piddles.

And Mr. Piddles looked like a man who was in no mood whatsoever to endure a temper tantrum/meltdown from a spoiled little blond-haired, middle school brat.

Just then I felt bad for Kiki. Really bad. I mean, it was, like, so obvious that she was under this huge amount of pressure to win. And she was crumbling from it. Cracking apart. Being the youngest sister in a family full of ThreePees who had already won the contest year after year after year must have made her feel as if the weight of the world was on her to win first place as well.

Buncha freaks.

But if she lost, she'd be the biggest disappointment in the history of her family. Didn't her mom or sisters see how much stress this was putting on "Keeks"? She looked thin and tired and drawn. There were even dark circles under her eyes. For an eighth grader, that's not good. Really, the signs were like, so obvious. The stress of this thing was turning her into a monster.

Everyone waited. Was Kiki about to have a major-league meltdown? Totally explode? Was she about to get her team disqualified by flipping out and completely self-destructing the day before the show? My shoulders got tense waiting to see what was going to happen.

Suddenly, and I don't know what it was, but suddenly, Kiki's brain started to function again, and she realized that Mr. Piddles was not a man to be messed with, so she zipped her lip, stormed off the stage, and shot about ten zillion daggers in the direction of Sofes O'Reilly.

Not a peep came from anyone for an awkwardly long time.

"Okay, Nerd Girls, you're up," said Mr. Piddles, taking his seat once again. "Please take the stage."

Our hearts jumped in our chests. With all the drama between Mr. Piddles and Kiki, I had forgotten that we still needed to perform.

We stood, gulped, and slowly took our positions. I set down Poochy and turned on the power switch.

"Just like at Beanpole's house," I said quietly. "Just like at Beanpole's. Think positive and let's rock this thing."

Beanpole smiled. I smiled. Poochy smiled. But not Q: she didn't smile at all. Instead, she suddenly began walking off the stage, just seconds before we were about to begin.

Oh no, I thought. Oh no.

However, before I could panic, Q set down her scuba tank, turned around, and returned to join us.

Then she smiled.

And we rocked it!

Absolutely nailed it! Did the best we had ever done. We made all our marks, hit all our steps, and had smiles on our faces the whole time. That really counts for something, too, when you're performing. Basically, we just laughed and danced and enjoyed ourselves.

And Poochy was, of course, a total star. He worked perfectly.

Then, we got to the final moment, and Poochy took his pee on the fire hydrant in the center of the stage. I turned and saw Mr. Piddles laughing so hard I thought he might end up peeing his pants. He loved it!

"Outstanding, Nerd Girls. Outstanding," he said at the end of our performance, clapping his hands together. "Tomorrow night should be a lot of fun."

He stood and grabbed his papers.

"Okay, everyone, that's a wrap. See you at the show."

I turned and looked off to the side of the stage. Kiki Masters was staring at me with rage in her eyes. I mean genuine hate.

I smiled back and gave her a little wave.

Like a package of chocolate pudding, I thought.

The three of us gathered our stuff and went out to the Fountain, where we let out an explosion of energy. We were so jazzed up it was like electrical currents were running through our veins.

"That was incredible!" said Beanpole, jumping up and down. "I can't believe how much fun that was."

"We did great," said Q. "Great!"

"We were awesome!" I said. "The Nerd Girls rocked it!"

"At first I was nervous but then it was fun," said Q. "Really fun."

I'd never seen Beanpole this perky. "I mean, when I did that one move, and then turned to bend down like this, and... OUCH!"

She smashed her head into the edge of the Fountain so hard, I was surprised that she hadn't knocked herself unconscious.

"Don't worry, don't worry, I'm okay," she said, barely fazed by the impact.

I looked at her forehead. She had a bump the size of Texas.

"Well, I guess things are back to normal," I said with a laugh.

Beanpole and Q smiled.

"Oh, I wouldn't get too excited yet, dork squad," came a mean and nasty voice from behind us. We turned and saw Kiki and her donkeys approaching. They looked fierce.

"One lucky practice round doesn't mean squat."

"Well, at least we finished our 'lucky' practice round," I answered. "But that was a great half-performance you guys gave. Really tremendous."

Everyone looked at Sofes. She lowered her eyes.

"Just don't forget, Nerd Girls," said Kiki, focusing her attention back on us, "that when the lights come up tomorrow, and the auditorium is full, there will be almost a thousand people in the audience."

"Yeah, a thousand people," repeated Brattany.

"The whole theater is going to be full, and let me tell you, it's a whole lot different than a little dress rehearsal, when the place is empty." Kiki's laugh had an evil tone in it. "And when the curtain comes up and the lights go down, all of these people will be watching."

Kiki pointed to Q.

"Watching you!"

"Yeah, watching you," said Brittany-Brattany, also pointing at Q.

I shook my head.

"What, are we back to the intimidation games again?" I said. *Geesh*, didn't we just prove to the ThreePees that their strategy of messing with our minds wasn't going to work?

"Hey, allergy freak, have you ever been onstage in front of one thousand people and had the lights go out in the middle of your performance?" asked Kiki.

Q's forehead started to wrinkle.

"Or had one of those HUGE spotlights shine directly in your eyes with such brightness that you couldn't see a stupid thing?" said Brattany.

Q slightly gulped.

"Or maybe," added Kiki, "you slipped on a part of the stage that had mysteriously become extra waxy just before you started your routine and fell so hard on your butt that the entire auditorium laughed and laughed and laughed at you?"

Q's eyes grew big and fearful. Clearly Kiki was getting to her.

"You know, all kinds of weird things can happen at showtime," said Kiki. "All kinds of weird, embarrassing, give-a-person-stage-fright, no-one-knows-how-they-happened type of things."

"Don't listen to her, Alice," said Beanpole. "We're going to be right there with you, and nothing's going to happen."

"Yeah," I said. "Nothing other than the fact that we are going to win."

"Of course," said Kiki in a sarcastic tone. "What could happen? I mean, it's not like the people who will be operating the lights are being paid by my mother or anything."

I paused.

"Didn't think about that, did you, chunky butt?" said Kiki.

"Yeah, and it's not like the fireworks people don't occasionally accept tips to do a little favor for clients who are extra generous with their money," said Brattany.

The two of them smiled like devils.

"No," said Kiki. "No reason to be nervous at all," she said in a voice dripping with sarcasm. "If I were you, I'd expect everything to go just fine tomorrow night. Just totally fine."

I stared at Kiki. She stared back, then turned her attention to Q.

"Just remember, disease-o," said Kiki. "Your worst fear might happen to you on stage tomorrow night, and we're all going to be there with cameras to make sure you never, ever, ever live it down."

"Yeah," said Brittany-Brattany. "If I were you, I wouldn't even show up."

"BOO!" said Kiki as she jumped at Q, scaring her half to death. Q practically popped out of her shoes. Kiki laughed.

"See ya tomorrow, Nerd Girls," cackled Kiki, and then the ThreePees walked back inside the Performing Arts Center. "We're just gonna go make a few *extra* preparations for the show," she said as they disappeared inside the auditorium in a secret, no-one-knows-we-are-in-here type of way.

A moment later, they were gone. Vanished. The three of us sat silent for a minute.

"They're gonna get us," said Q.

"They're not going to get us," I said.

"I just know it. They're gonna get us," Q replied.

"Calm down," I said. "They're all talk. They're not going to get us."

"Yes they are," said Q, growing more and more nervous. "They always do. They're gonna get us, and they are going to embarrass me, and they are going to make me feel like a loser in front of all these people who are going to laugh, and then it'll be just like it always is whenever I try to do something right, and the world hates me and I end up being put into situations I can't handle, and then the screams are going to start and the blood and the fire and all the metal and glass flying and—"

"Whoa, whoa, calm down, Q. Calm down," I said. "You're rambling. Take a deep breath and relax."

Q took a few slurps off the scuba tank, but she had that far-away look in her eyes again, the one that came from that weirdo place inside of her.

Just then, we heard a car horn.

"Ugh, the picture?" said Beanpole.

"What picture?" I said.

I looked out at the parking lot. It was Beanpole's parents coming to pick her up.

"My dad," she replied. "He's taking us to go get our family picture taken by that professional photographer today. I totally forgot."

She turned and called out to her parents. "One minute," She turned to Q. "You all right?"

Q didn't respond.

"Alice, you all right?" Beanpole asked again. "I mean, I can stay or give you a ride home or something."

"No, I..." Q paused. "I'd rather walk."

"You sure?" asked Beanpole. "I mean, are you gonna be okay?"

"She's gonna be fine," I said, thinking that if I encouraged her enough, Q would turn into that Wild West gunfighter once again. All I needed was a few minutes of applying some positive talk and she'd be just ready to go. I was sure of it.

"She'll be fine," I repeated. " 'Cause there's nothing to worry about. The ThreePees aren't going to be able to hurt us. Come on, think about it. Mr. Piddles wouldn't allow it."

"How do you know?" said Q.

"Because," I said, "it wouldn't be..." I paused. "Just."

Q and Beanpole looked at me with wrinkled foreheads.

"It wouldn't be just," I repeated.

Talk about a good time to come up with a good answer. I don't know how it happened, but I seemed to get really lucky with that one, because suddenly, both Q and Beanpole realized I was probably right, and the tension started to disappear on Q's face.

"They might be mean and nasty, but the ThreePees don't own the school," I said. "They don't get to control everything."

The car horn honked again. Department Store Dad pointed to his watch.

"One minute," Beanpole yelled. "One minute."

"I mean, come on, they're not going to be able to put extra wax on the floor or make paint cans fall on our heads or anything like that," I said. "Think about it. It's stupid. The only reason they're trying to scare us is because they're scared."

"They are, aren't they?" said Q.

"Of course they are," I answered. "And they should be. I mean, Sofes is in eighth grade and she still doesn't know her left from her right. That might be a Guinness World Record or something."

Beanpole and Q laughed. The car horn honked for a third time.

"G'head, Beanpole," I said. "Go take your picture, and we'll all meet at Q's tomorrow and drive on over in the Nerd Mobile. I'll stay with the basket case here till her mom comes."

"You sure?" said Beanpole. "'Cause I can wait."

"It's okay, go," I said. "I wouldn't want your dad's sweater to start bunching up on him."

"Well…" said Beanpole, thinking about it, "okay. But be nice to her," she said to me.

"I'm always nice, ya doof-brain string bean! Now go," I said.

"Okay, see you tomorrow," said Beanpole, giving Q a big hug.

Then she hugged me too.

"Um…yeah…okay…awkward," I said. I kinda weirdly half hugged her back.

"See you guys," said Beanpole, grabbing her backpack. "Tomorrow at your house, Alice."

"Bye," said Q.

"See ya, Beanpole," I called out. "And watch out for the—"

"Ouch!"

"Bicycle racks."

"Don't worry, I'm okay. I'm okay," said Beanpole as she picked herself up off the pavement and got into the car. A minute later the Department Store Family drove off. I turned to Q.

"You okay?" I asked.

"Yeah," she said. "Better."

"Okay, then wait here. I gotta pee."

"Hydrating?" Q smiled.

"Like you don't even know," I answered. "But when I come back, we'll talk about how stupid the ThreePees are and how we are going to smash them like a package of chocolate pudding, okay?"

Q sat down on the ledge of the fountain. "Okay," she said, looking more calm.

"And if you want," I said, coming up with a great idea, "talk to Poochy. I'll leave him right here." I took off my backpack and set it down at Q's feet. "He's not just a good dancer, ya know, he's a good listener, too. Tell him all your weirdo problems, and I am sure he'll give you great advice."

Q looked up at me. "Thanks, Maureen." There was a tear in her eye. "I mean, well…thanks."

"For what?" I said.

"For, well, I hope you know that…I just don't want to let you down."

"Let me down?"

"Yeah, let you down," she said. "I mean, I know I am a loser and people are going to pick on me for the rest of my life, but you, well, you could be"—she struggled to find the right word—"accepted."

"Accepted?" I said. "Are you sure you don't need a hit off the scuba tank or something? I don't think enough of those inhibitors are getting to your brain."

"Yeah," she said in a serious tone. "You could be accepted. I mean, I know I'll never be, but you, well... I just don't want to let you down."

"Look, you're not letting me down, you itchy-lipped, rash-faced freak-a-zoid." I hopped on one foot because *wow* did I really have to pee. "And don't go getting all emotional on me either. I mean, first Beanpole hugs me, and now you cry; next thing you know we'll be singing stupid songs together and writing dumb messages in one another's yearbooks."

Q took a slurp off the scuba tank. *Wheeesh-whooosh. Wheeesh-whooosh.* "You're funny."

"I'm not trying to be funny," I said. "Now, just stay here and stay strong for like five minutes, okay?" I added. "I'll be right back. I just really need to pee."

"Okay, go," Q answered. "I'll wait."

It'd been about two and a half hours since I last peed, probably the longest stretch of time since I'd started this dumb watch-what-I-eat, exercise, and-drink-a-lot-of-water thing. Actually, I shouldn't call it dumb because the truth was all this cuckoo health stuff was working. Though I didn't want to weigh myself because I always felt bad whenever I got on a scale, I knew I had lost some weight. I mean, all my pants were looser, my jeans didn't squeak so much when I walked through the halls, and I had to admit, I did feel a lot better about my body.

Not wanting to use the bathroom in the Performing Arts Center in case I ran into the ThreePees, I scooted back to the main part of campus and found a restroom by the science corridor, where I took a pee, washed my hands, and looked in the mirror.

Actually, I didn't just look in the mirror, I kinda talked to the mirror, too.

I talked about how it was "Revenge time." I talked to it about how "I looked good." I talked about how "Our act is good," about how "We have 'em where we want 'em," and about how "I finally have a chance to get back at the girls who have hurt me so bad for so long."

For the first time in my life, weird as this sounds, I really looked at myself in the mirror. And spoke to myself. Honestly, I talked to me.

Then I told myself one of the most truthful things I had ever said.

"Maybe I used to be one thing," I said. "But not anymore."

No more would I be a baked potato. No more would I be the girl who always got laughed at. No more would I be the sad little outcast who always felt picked on and bad about herself and thought she was an idiot-doofo-weirdo-turdhead loser.

No more would I hate myself. For the first time in a long, long time, I felt good.

Really good.

I walked out of the bathroom knowing that nothing was going to stop me. Nothing at all. Not food. Not fear of failure. Not the ThreePees.

Especially not the ThreePees.

I headed back to Q with a bounce in my step. By this time tomorrow night, there would be a new Maureen, one that that for the first time in her life not only felt good, but *was* good.

However, Q wasn't around.

"Q?" I said, calling out. "Hey, dorkwad, where'd ya go?"

There was no answer.

"Q?" I called again.

A voice startled me from behind.

"Looks like someone forgot to teach the little doggie how to swim."

Huh?

I looked at the Fountain. There, at the bottom of the pool, was Poochy.

What the...

I raised my eyes. In the distance I saw Q walking farther and farther away.

"Q!" I shouted. "Q!"

"I don't think she's gonna turn around," said Sofes, giggling. "Not after all that hyperescalating."

"Hyperventilating, Sofes," said Kiki. "The freak was hyperventilating."

"Same thing," she answered.

"Q!" I cried out again, but Sofes was right: Q was too far away, and even if she had heard me, she didn't look like she was going to turn around for anything.

I spun back around and looked at the bottom of the Fountain.

"See ya tomorrow, fat girl," laughed Kiki.

And with that, the ThreePees wiggled off.

I pulled Poochy from the bottom of the Fountain and lifted him up. Water drained out of his ear. I tried to turn on the power.

Nothing. The dog looked at me with an empty stare.

He was dead. Dead.

Totally and completely dead.

I put Poochy inside my backpack and zipped it tight. I was so stunned I felt numb. Emptiness filled me. I mean, you'd think I would have wanted to kill the ThreePees, or kill myself, but instead my insides were in a total state of shock. I just felt hollow, blah, gone. It was as if the complete disbelief of seeing Poochy in the Fountain had sucked my soul out of me like some sort of high-powered vacuum cleaner, and there didn't feel like there was anything else put back in its place. Though it would have been totally like me to do so, I didn't yell, stomp, scream, flip out, or explode.

And I didn't go snitch to a teacher, either. Why? Because

really, I realized as I shuffled away, it was all my fault. Really, it was all my own stupid fault.

I mean, why did I ever think I could be normal?

You're such a loser, Maureen, I thought. Such a total loser.

I headed home.

And partnering up with a bunch of other loser-weirdo freaks certainly doesn't help things either, now does it?

Like I said, *such a total loser.*

I dragged my feet forward like I was on automatic pilot. However, instead of going home, I made an unscheduled but completely mandatory detour.

To Paradise Palace.

"Seven of those, please," I said as I put some money on the counter.

"Eez there a cupcake party?" asked the guy behind the cash register when he saw all the two-packs of chocolate love I was purchasing.

"You could say that," I answered. Not only was the junk food junky at Paradise Palace, it was cheap too. For just a few bucks a person could stuff their face completely.

"Hey," I added, suddenly pointing to the long pieces of rubber turning around and around under the heat lamps, shimmering in grease. "How are those hot dogs?"

"Dee-lee-cious," the guy answered. "I eet two or three a day."

"You know, I've always wanted to try one," I said.

"So, you vood like?" he asked.

I paused and considered what I was about to put into my body. "On second thought, naw," I answered.

He shrugged his shoulders as if to say, "Okay, you're the customer."

"Better gimme two," I said. "Need my nutrition, ya know."

He smiled, glad that I was joining his toxic-hot-dog-eating club.

"Weeeth relish?" he asked, grabbing some tongs.

"And kraut and cheese and chili bacon, too," I answered. "Load 'em up."

"Youz got eet," he said.

I paid for my food, grabbed my convenience-store death dogs, and got ready to walk out. However, there wasn't enough room in my backpack for all the cupcakes as well as Poochy, at least not without squishing all of the tasty, delectable treats.

Hmm, what to do, I thought.

"Excuse me, is there a garbage?" I asked.

The man pointed to a bin under the Icee machine. I walked over and—*BOOM!*—dropped Poochy into the gray can.

Good, I thought. Plenty of room in my backpack now.

"Hey," said the convenience store guy as I was walking away. "Eez too beeg. You no can throw there."

"What?"

"Eez too big," he repeated, pointing at Poochy. "Take oop too much room. Take weeth you, take weeth you."

Frustrated, I shrugged my shoulders and picked up Poochy from out of the garbage can. Whoever heard of there being rules to what you could throw away in a convenience store? I looked at my backpack, still not wanting to smash my cupcakes.

Hmm, what to do?

"Do you have a Phillips head?" I asked.

"A vutt?"

"A Phillips head? A Phillips head screwdriver?" I said.

"A pheeleeps heed, no," he answered. "Just a reegular head."

He held up a long screwdriver.

"That'll do," I said. "Can I borrow it for a sec?"

"Sure theeng." He passed me the screwdriver. With a Phillips head I would have been able to unscrew some of the pieces, but with a flat head, I wasn't really able to turn any of the screws without stripping them, so instead of properly disassembling the robotic dog, I simply jammed the screwdriver deep into Poochy's neck.

Then popped off his head.

"There," I said, handing the man his screwdriver. "Thanks."

"You braked it," the guy said to me, seeing the damage I had done to the dog.

"It was already braked," I told him. "In a way, I guess you could say the whole idea of it was braked a long, long time ago."

I stuffed Poochy's head and body into my bag. Now that the dog had been decapitated, I was easily able to fit all the pieces into my backpack without smashing any of the cupcakes.

Perfect, I thought. I mean, you gotta have priorities, right?

I picked up my chili-bacon death dogs off the counter, took a big bite, and made sure that all the performers in the cupcake carnival were tucked safely away in a smush-proof place in my backpack.

"Eez good?" the guy asked after I plowed a huge hunk of overcooked mystery meat into my face hole.

"Eez dee-lee-cious," I answered. "Thanks. See ya tomorrow."

"Too-mahrroo?" he asked.

"Yeah, too-mahrroo," I answered. "What, you don't work?"

"No," he replied. "I'll bee heer."

"So wlll I," I answered. "So will I."

Then I walked home.

"How was it, Boo?" asked my mom as I came through the front door. Both Ashley and Marty looked up when I entered.

Just then I did the best acting job ever done on the face of the planet. It was like I deserved ten Academy Awards for my performance.

"It was awesome, Mom," I said with all the perkiness of Beanpole. "Just awesome! We hit all our marks, and Poochy was great, and the judge even laughed out loud at the end. You were, like, so right. Being positive is the secret. I'm always going to be positive from now on."

"That's excellent," she said, thrilled to hear the news.

"We really nailed it. One thousand percent," I added. Then I burped. It tasted like burned bacon chili. *Gross.*

"Where's the dog?" asked Marty, reaching for my backpack. "I want to check him out and make sure he's all set."

I pulled my bag away before he could get to it.

"He's fine," I said. "Just fine. But Q wanted to take him home. You know how she can be sometimes. I figured it was good for her self-esteem. For all I know, she's cuddling with Poochy on the couch right now."

My mom laughed.

"But . . ." said Marty, noticing that my bag was pretty full for a person who wasn't carrying a robotic dog around.

"Oh, relax, Poochy is great," I said, cutting Marty off. "A real champ. You know, I think we're gonna win tomorrow," I announced.

"You do?" said my mom, happily surprised by the idea of it.

"I do," I said. "I really, really do."

My mother beamed with so much pride I thought her cheeks were going to explode. Marty, however, still looked suspicious.

"I'm gonna go shower, then get to sleep early so I can be well rested for the performance tomorrow," I said.

"No dinner?" asked my mom. "I made a healthy salad."

"Naw," I answered. "I'm not hungry."

"Nerves?" she asked.

"Probably," I replied.

"It's natural," she said, trying to be supportive.

"I guess," I said casually. "Oh, Mom," I added.

"Yeah, Boo?"

"You're not going to be mad if we don't exercise in the morning, are you? I think I want to sleep in."

My mother paused and then smiled even bigger.

"I think we can afford to take a day off," she answered. "We've earned it, don't you think?"

"You're the best, Mom," I said. "Just the best."

I turned to head for my room, but Marty suspected something was up.

"Aw, you gotta think positive, bro," I said before I walked away. "Everything's gonna be great tomorrow. Just spek-tak-cu-lar!"

Ashlee looked at me with a twisted expression on her face.

"And you," I said before bouncing up the stairs, "your hair

looks really cute like that. You should wear it that way more often."

"It does?" she said.

"Really, it does," I answered. "Brings out your cheekbones. Are all your friends still coming to show their support?"

"Um, yeah," Ashley answered.

I went to my bedroom, closed the door, and began to eat.

And eat and eat and eat. It was just me and the chocolate love parade starring Mr. Cupcake and all his talented friends.

And really, why not? I mean, no matter what I did, I would always be one of life's losers. Nothing would ever change that. No matter how hard I tried, no matter how much effort I gave, no matter how long I worked or how good I attempted to be, I had just learned the most valuable lesson the world could ever offer.

In this life, there are winners and losers; and me, I was a loser. A big, fat loser. Always had been, always would be.

Always.

It was a fact that only chocolate cupcakes understood. Lucky for me I had fourteen of them to help get me through the night.

The more I chewed and thought and chewed and thought and swallowed, the more I realized that I should actually be thanking Kiki and the ThreePees for what they had just taught me. I mean, think about how many people never learn the lesson that they are one of life's nothings in this world, and waste all their precious years trying and trying to be something they are not. Like a cat will always be a cat, and a dog will always be a dog, and a ferret will always be a ferret.

But a ferret will never be a cat or a dog, no matter what it does, right?

Me, I'd always be a ferret, and in a way, the ThreePees had just saved me all the stupid effort of ever trying to be a dog or a cat again.

I closed my eyes and fell asleep, dreaming ferret dreams and preparing for a ferret tomorrow. I don't even remember taking off my stupid watch before climbing into my stupid bed.

The next morning I woke up with the taste of chocolate on my tongue. *Urgh!* I had forgotten to brush my teeth. And as everyone knows, the only way to cure the taste of unbrushed chocolate on your tongue is with...

More chocolate. But I need fresh stuff.

Paradise Palace, here I come!

I headed downstairs.

"Big day today, Boo," said my mom, sipping her cup of coffee.

"Uh-huh," I replied.

"Where you goin'?" she asked.

"For a walk," I said. "You know, clear my head."

"Want company?"

"No thanks," I said. "I think I am gonna stop by Q's house for a minute anyway."

"Sort of a pep talk before the big show?" she asked.

"Exactly, Mom," I answered. "You nailed it."

I faked a big, happy, positive smile and left. Then it hit me: I *should* go to Q's house. Not to give her a big pep talk. Of course not; why would I want to do that? But to tell her the truth.

The real truth.

The truth about how we couldn't hang around at lunch anymore. Or after school. Or in the halls or at any of our houses or anything.

Of course I expected Q to start explaining to me about all her lame-o-ness. About how it wasn't her fault, about how the ThreePees outnumbered her, about how when she had one of her famous hyperventilating, freak-out, "oh no, I'm panicking!" attacks and dropped to her knees to put her hands over her head in order to catch her breath, the ThreePees stole the dog from her and threw it in the Fountain. Walking over to her house, I just knew that Q'd probably have a sad little excuse for everything.

A sad little excuse with a whole lot of *Wheeesh-whooosh, Wheeesh-whooosh* sound effects mixed in, too. What a mutant.

But really, did excuses even matter? I mean, what difference did it make how it happened? All that mattered was Poochy was dead, we had lost, and once again, dorkwads like us were going to be life's losers.

Maybe I should have snitched? I mean, I could have snitched. Could have told the teachers and the parents and the whole world everything. But really, what was the point? I'd still be a ferret, a loser, a Nerd Girl, and there wasn't anything that was going to change that. If I tattled to a teacher or a parent, it would have been just like setting myself up to lose again.

Naw, it was over. Everything was completely and totally over. After all, I had been born on Planet Piece-of-Garbageville, and no one can ever change where they were born.

Nope, I was going to Q's house for a different reason. I was going to Q's house to tell her that it was like I had always said it would be, that the best that Allergy Alice, Beanpole Barbara, and Big-Boned Maureen, the Human Baked Potato, could ever possibly be was associated grapes.

And I wanted to disassociate.

Over. Done. No more.

I just wanted to live my life at the bottom of life's grape bowl all by myself.

Forget the talent show. Forget the ThreePees. Forget one another. I was better off in this world as a lonely, shriveled grape.

Okay, a plump grape. But either way, a grape that wasn't associated.

I walked up to Alice's front door. It was painted red, a sign for good luck.

Yeah, right, I thought.

Associations caused pain. Associations caused disappointment. Associations caused humiliation. It was time to, once again, become disassociated. Better for everyone that way.

I knocked. Mrs. Applebee, Alice's mother answered.

That's when things changed forever.

So this is where the kook-job lives, I thought as the door opened.

"Hello?"

"Is Q...I mean, your daughter, is she home?" I asked in a short voice.

"Well, you must be Maureen," said Q's mom, welcoming me inside with a warm smile. "Please, come in. I'm glad we finally get to meet."

I entered and looked around. The house seemed normal enough...for a freak asylum, that is.

"Alice is resting right now before the big show," said Mrs. Applebee. "Can I offer you something to drink?"

"Naw," I said. I just wanted to get in and get out and then hit Paradise Palace on the way home. It would be jelly doughnut day for me. One for the history books.

"Please, sit down, sit down," Q's mom instructed. I tried to look down the hallway to see the psycho girl's bedroom, but her mother had me copping a squat on the couch before I could get a good peek.

She took a seat across from me in a blue chair. Oh great, it was talk-with-another-kid's-mom time.

"You know, I can't tell you how happy I am that Alice finally has some real friends," she began. Her smile was wide and bright.

"Uh-huh," I replied, not really in the mood for chitchat.

"I mean, this is Alice's third school in two years," she continued. "It's like everyone shuns her, and she can't..." Mrs. Applebee paused. "It's like she can't fit in."

"Um, yeah," I said. "Is she gonna be awake any time soon so that I can..."

"Kids can be just so mean to one another," Q's mom said, finishing her own thought more than she was answering me.

"You can say that again," I responded.

"The meanest," she added. "Just absolutely cruel."

Mrs. Applebee shook her head from side to side. There was a pause. I tried to look down the hall.

"Um, do you know if she's gonna..."

"I mean, just because Alice thinks she killed her father and sister doesn't mean that she's a bad person, but I can't get that message through to her."

WHAT? My head snapped back around.

"I shouldn't say *killed*," Alice's mom said, correcting herself. "What's that my therapist says? I should say, 'feels responsible for the untimely passing of.' See, words have power. They have the power to..."

Q's mom stopped mid-sentence. Her hands began to shake.

"That accident, it ruined my life. It ruined our lives."

Mrs. Applebee began to cry.

What accident? I thought.

"Okay, so Alice was misbehaving in the backseat," she continued in a rambling, talking-to-herself, trying-to-figure-it-all-out type of way. "Big deal. She was eleven years old and wanted the video game back from her younger sister. Does that mean Alice *killed* her family? Of course not."

Tearful, she shook her head.

"And I told her, sisters fight all the time, and it was raining, and just because my husband had to turn around to stop them from arguing doesn't mean that she's responsible for the crash. But she doesn't believe me."

Tears streamed down her face.

"She thinks it's her fault her father and sister are dead."

I couldn't help but think about how many times my sister and I had fought in the backseat of the car while my mom was trying to drive.

"I mean, losing my husband and daughter has been the hardest thing in the world for me, but now, it's like I'm losing Alice too. Losing her to guilt."

She reached for a tissue and wiped her eyes.

"They call it survivor's guilt," she continued. "Though her father and sister died in the accident, Alice walked away without any serious injuries. Just a few cuts and bruises. A real miracle. But Alice wishes she had died instead of them. She feels so bad about what happened, she wishes she could trade places with them, to make things even, somehow."

The room became weirdly quiet. I didn't know what to say.

"Tell me, how is a kid supposed to handle that?" Q's mom asked, as if I somehow had the answer. "She didn't mean for it to happen. She didn't do it on purpose. I love her. Why should she have to suffer more than she already has?"

Mrs. Applebee reached for another tissue.

"Okay, so she misses a few days of school now and then. But it's the stress. She was always allergic to peanuts and cow's milk, but ever since the crash, her allergies have just gone haywire. And the doctors, well, those geniuses have no explanation," she added. "No explanation other than all the pressure and anxiety. Alice, she's one of those types that keeps it all bottled up."

Mrs. Applebee blew her nose.

"But she's normal, right? She's not a freak. She's just a young girl trying to handle an impossible situation, and for the life of me, I don't understand why so many kids at her school are so insensitive and mean to her."

I looked down.

"Don't they know? Don't they see how badly she's hurting on the inside?"

Mrs. Applebee again began to cry. Really cry, like a deep weep.

"Don't they know how badly all of us are hurting on the inside?"

Q's mom went on weeping for two solid minutes without saying anything. All she did was cry. Me, I just sat there staring, not knowing what to say or do, scared to even move. It was like Alice's mom had been carrying around this giant sadness for so long, and suddenly, somehow, I was the one who had opened the faucet that allowed her tears to flow.

"Oh, jeez," she finally said, waking out of a weepy daze. "Look at me, I'm a mess."

She tried to wipe her face, but mascara was smudged everywhere.

"You're a good friend, Maureen," she said, taking me by the hand. I wanted to yank my hand back, but I couldn't seem to move. The look on Mrs. Applebee's face changed from one of sadness to one of fierce determination.

"A real friend. A true friend. She talks about how funny you are all the time."

I gulped.

"I mean, I was scared Alice was going to try to keep this hidden from everyone for the rest of her life, but for her to have told you all about it, well ... it really says a lot about the kind of person you are. You and Barbara. She's lucky to have you."

I stared, silent and motionless.

"And the truth is," she added, "I just don't know where she'd be without you."

Mrs. Applebee grabbed two more tissues. By the time this conversation was done, she was going to need a whole new box.

"Funny, but I guess Alice finally decided to listen to her therapist when he said that if she keeps it all hush-hush and secret for the rest of her life, it will eat her up and destroy her. I guess it just took the right person to connect with her and bring it out."

Mrs. Applebee lifted her head and looked me in the eyes.

"You are a good egg, Maureen," she said. "I knew from the moment Alice started telling me about you that you were a good egg. That's rare in this world. Rare indeed."

Q's mom took a breath and gathered herself.

"By the way, can I tell you how excited she is about tonight?" she said, shifting gears into a more happy direction. "I mean, I haven't seen Alice this hopeful and excited since, well...since before."

I stared at my shoes.

"That accident has shaped every aspect of our lives," she added. "Every last part of it. That is, until you and Barbara came along. And now, tonight, for the first time in years, Alice gets to be normal. She gets to be a regular kid. Funny, but I think we were both scared that she had lost that forever."

I couldn't even lift my eyes.

"She's napping because she needs her strength for this evening, but, well"—Mrs. Applebee paused—"I think it's going to be a real breakthrough for her tonight. A real breakthrough."

"Uh, yeah," I said sort of stupidly.

"And no matter how you do, at least you'll do it together," she continued. "As friends. And sometimes in life, well...that's all we really need. Friends are everything. Especially when times get tough.

"Oh yeesh, look at me crying and blabbering on." She stood. "I can't sit here like this. Will you excuse me a minute, please?"

"Uh, sure," I said.

Mrs. Applebee smoothed out her blouse.

"Are you sure you don't want anything to drink?" she asked, wiping her eyes again. "Something to eat?"

"Um, no. I'm fine."

"Well, if you change your mind, the kitchen is right in there. Help yourself, I'll be right back." Q's mom walked away.

I sat there, alone in the living room, absolutely stunned. A part of me wanted to run. To flee. To head for the front door and get out of that house as fast as possible.

But then I saw a picture on the mantel. It was a picture of Q and her dad, both wearing mouse ears.

I went up to get a closer look. They were at Disneyland, the Happiest Place on Earth, and I could tell by the looks on their faces that there wasn't a daughter alive who loved her dad more than Q had loved hers.

Or a dad who had loved his daughter just as much. They say some pictures are worth a thousand words. This one was worth twenty bazillion words. The smiles on their faces said it all.

But the man in the picture was dead. And the little girl in the picture next to him, the one with the bright face and the missing front teeth and the pigtails, she was dead too.

And Q thought it was all her fault. The whole thing, her fault. Wow.

"Are you sure I can't get you anything?" asked Alice's mother, returning to the room. She startled me. "Not even a glass of water? Alice tells me you've been drinking a lot of it lately."

"Uh, no," I said, quickly turning around. "No thanks. I... I gotta go."

"I, um, hope it's nothing I said," she answered. "I didn't mean to—"

"No, no, not at all," I replied. "I just really need to, you know, get home."

"Was there something you came over for?" she asked. "I thought I remember Alice telling me that we weren't going to be taking the Nerd Mobile over to school till about three thirty, and it's only about one right now. The Nerd Mobile." She laughed. "You girls are too funny."

"Reason I came over?" I said. "Uh, no. I mean, yes. Well, no. I only came over to, uh..." I started to stutter. "To give Alice a pep talk. You know, stay positive, that's all. I mean, I guess she hasn't told you about tonight, has she?"

I studied Mrs. Applebee's face for a clue.

"Told me what?" Q's mom asked.

"About"—I paused, trying to read her thoughts—"the show?"

Mrs. Applebee casually shook her head. She had no idea what I was talking about.

"No, nothing special. I mean, Alice came home last night, skipped dinner, and pretty much went straight to her room. I think she might have watched a little TV, but no, she didn't say anything. I just figured she was nervous, you know, about the big performance. Why, did something happen?"

"Happen?" I said. "Um, no, what would have happened? No, nothing happened. Nothing at all." I bent down and retied my shoe even though it didn't need it. "Yeah, I gotta go," I said when I stood back up. "Bye," I said, making my way for the front door.

"Are you sure that—"

"Totally sure," I answered. "I just...I gotta go. Bye."

And with that I left.

I wandered around for a little while, not really knowing where to go or what to do. Without me even telling them to do so, my feet walked me back to Paradise Palace. But I didn't go in. Doughnuts and chili dogs didn't seem like the answer. I didn't know what the answer was, my brain was just so dang cloudy, but food wasn't singing any love songs to me. Finally, after wandering around some more, I wandered back home.

"Hey, Boo," said my mom as I walked through the front door.

"Hey," I answered in a low voice.

"You thinking positive?" she said, trying to make sure I was still feeling energized about tonight.

"Mm, just thinking," I said.

"Well, that's better than not thinking, I guess," she said with a laugh.

I approached the kitchen table where she was sitting. My mom was trying to hide something, but I could see a piece of silky red ribbon.

It was a bouquet of roses. Obviously, they were for me.

For later.

"You weren't supposed to see those," she said with a smile.

I bent over to smell them.

"Mmm, good," I said. No one had ever bought me roses before.

I looked at my mom. She looked back at me. We made eye contact, and I knew I was going to have to tell her. I lowered my eyes and opened my mouth to speak.

"Mom," I said softly. "I . . ."

I paused.

"Yes, Boo?" she said.

"I . . . I'll be in my room."

I stood up. I just didn't know what to say or how to say it.

I turned to head upstairs. However, I could feel my mother's eyes staring at me.

"Hey, Maureen."

"Yes, Mom," I answered.

"I'm proud of you," she said. "No matter what happens tonight, I'm proud of you, Boo."

I could feel the teardrops starting to swell in my eyes.

"Mom..." I turned back around. "I don't think there's going to be a—"

Ding-dong! Suddenly, the doorbell rang. My mother, excited as an eight-year-old who was getting a pony for Christmas, popped out of her chair, bubbling with energy.

"Delivery!" she cried out in a singsong voice.

Delivery? I thought.

My mom threw open the door, and standing there was a man holding a giant box.

"Saunders residence?"

"This way, this way," said my mom, leading him inside. "Just put it down right there," she told him. Then she looked at me.

"I figured we'd have a few people over after the show to celebrate," she said. "With chocolate! Yum!" She threw open the box.

It was a cake.

"After all, we haven't had chocolate in about eight hundred years, and you only live once, right?" she said with a big, mischievous smile.

"Just sign here, please, ma'am," said the delivery man, holding his clipboard.

My mom signed and looked inside the big box.

"You weren't really supposed to see this either, but what the hey," she told me. "I was always terrible at keeping secrets and surprises and stuff like that anyway."

My mom giggled. She was having so much fun.

"What were you going to say about tonight, Boo?" she asked as she swiped a taste of frosting from the side of the cake. Couldn't help herself, I guess.

"Um," I replied. I looked inside the box. The cake read CONGRATULATIONS NERD GIRLS! in pink-and-yellow frosting. And wow, was it big. There must have been enough to feed an entire neighborhood's worth of people.

Just then I realized that my mom probably had invited an entire neighborhood's worth of people over, too, including the Department Store Parents, Alice's mother, everyone up and down the block, and probably a whole bunch of other folks as well. With a cake this big, who wouldn't be coming back to our house after the performance?

"Nothing, Mom," I said softly. "Nothing. Wasn't important."

That's when it dawned on me. This was the first time in my whole life that my mother really felt she had good reason to be proud of me, genuinely proud of me.

Me, I just didn't have the heart to tell her that it wasn't going to happen; that her little Boo was once again going to come home empty-handed.

Like they say, when it rains, it pours.

"Here, take a taste, Boo," my mother said, eagerly, scooping up a dash of frosting onto her fingertip. "I know you haven't had any sweets in a while, but you are gonna love this. Double chocolate fudge with a molten chocolate middle. *Mmm*. They call this cake Sin-n-Guilt, the double-whammy specialty of the house," she said, beaming with joy.

I looked at the swirl of frosting on her fingertip waiting for my tongue.

"Homemade buttercream," she said, tempting me a bit more. "I mean, if you're going to swim in a pool, you might as well jump into the deep end, right?"

I stared and thought about what to do.

"Um, no thanks, Mom," I said.

"Are you sure, Boo?" she asked.

I looked at the cake again.

Am I sure? I thought. To tell the truth, all I wanted to do at that very moment was dive into the cake box and not stop gobbling until there was nothing left but cardboard and tape.

But what I wanted to do and what I needed to do, well... they were two different things.

Two different things entirely. I turned to walk away.

"Where're you going, Boo?"

"I need to speak with Marty," I said.

And with that, I went upstairs.

"Knock-knock," I said, tapping on my brother's door.

"Yeah?" he answered. "Come in."

I entered carrying my backpack.

"Pink or green?" my brother asked when he saw me.

"Huh?" I said.

"Which'll look better with this yellow shirt? Pink or green?" He held out two neckties.

"Why're you wearing a tie?" I asked.

"Mom's making me," he answered. "And you should see

Ashley's dress. It's like she's going to a wedding or something. So which one, pink or green?"

"Uh, green," I said, mindlessly.

"Not the pink?" he asked.

"Okay, pink," I answered. "Look, I have to—"

"Come on, Maureen," said Marty, interrupting me. "I mean, after all I've done for you, the least you could do is help me choose a dumb tie."

I paused. He was right. Slowly, I turned and studied the choices.

"Okay, hypothetically speaking," I said, inspecting both of the options. "What color do you feel most comfortable in?"

"Green," he answered, holding up the green tie.

"And hypothetically speaking," I continued, "what color would make the biggest, most bold fashion statement?" I asked.

"Pink," he replied, holding up the other tie.

"All right, then hypothetically speaking," I continued, "if Poochy were drowned in a fountain filled with chlorinated water, do you think you could get him back to normal in forty-five minutes?"

"What?"

"Hypothetically speaking, of course." I unzipped my backpack and dumped Poochy parts all over the floor. "Well, maybe not so hypothetically."

Marty's eyes practically bugged out of his head.

"What happened?" he said, inspecting the damage.

"They threw it in the Fountain," I answered.

"They threw it in the Fountain? The girls from your school?" Marty held up Poochy's head. Water dribbled out of its ear. "He's ruined."

"But you can fix him, right?"

"No," Marty answered. "He's ruined."

"But he's fixable?" I said. "I mean, you can get some thingies back together so that—"

"No," Marty said, cutting me off. "He's ruined, Maureen. Done. Zapped. Destroyed."

He lifted up Poochy's body by the tail. More water dribbled onto the floor. Marty hopelessly shook his head.

"It's totally toast."

I paused and thought for a minute.

"Marty, if you think positive, you can—"

"Don't sound like Mom," he interrupted.

"Well, don't sound like Dad," I snapped back.

Marty glared. "That was low, Maureen. Like totally below the belt."

He dropped the dog and turned to walk out of the room.

I jumped in front of him, blocking his path. "Wait, I'm sorry."

He continued to glare.

"Really, I'm sorry," I said again. "But you have to fix it, Marty. Please," I begged. "Like, you don't understand."

"Maureen, you don't get it. This thing is totally—"

"I mean I really, really, really need you to fix it," I said. "Like more than you'll ever know."

I started to cry.

"Please, Marty," I said. "For Alice."

"What? Why for Alice?" he asked.

"I . . . I can't tell you," I answered.

"Uh, hello," he said. "Like, is this really the time for stupid little kiddie secrets?"

"I don't know what it's time for," I replied. "But I do know that one way or another we have to go to that show tonight, and like, it would be really, really helpful to have a dancing robot dog to join us."

"I don't get it," he said. "You're making it sound like life or death."

"Please," I said softly. "Don't use that word."

He stared.

"You're weird," Marty said.

"Just fix the dog," I said. "Please, fix the dog."

I exited Marty's bedroom, went to my room, and grabbed the sparkling pink outfit Department Store Mom had made for me. A moment later I walked back into Marty's room, having put together a last-ditch plan.

"I gotta get changed and back to Q's before Beanpole gets there," I said. "Fix Poochy best you can and meet me at the show, okay?"

Marty clearly didn't understand. A tear rolled down my cheek.

"It's a big one, Marty," I told him. "Like the biggest of all time. And I need you to come through."

I paused and waited for him to answer. Marty looked back at all the broken dog parts and shook his head.

"I'll try," he said. "I'll try."

"Cool, see you there," I told him, and then I headed down the stairs.

"But no promises, Maureen," he cried out as he gazed at the damaged dog. "Just so you know, no promises."

A moment later, I left for Q's house.

21

I knocked and knocked and knocked at Q's front door like a neighbor that had locked themselves out of their own house and really needed to use the bathroom. Alice answered wearing ugly green pajamas. She looked absolutely terrible.

"Get dressed," I said.

"What are you doing here?" she asked.

I pushed my way in through the front door and looked for Beanpole. No sign of her.

"He fixed it," I said. "Get dressed!"

"He didn't fix it," she said.

"He did," I answered. "Well, not fixed it yet, but he is fixing it. He's almost done."

Q paused and thought about what I'd just said.

"Nuh-unh," she said. "Impossible."

"It is possible," I told her. "And if he does fix it and we're not

188

there when he brings it to the show, how lame will it be to lose to the ThreePees that way, like a buncha chumps?"

Q thought about it, yet still she didn't budge.

"Would you please just go get dressed?" I said.

"It's not worth it, Maureen," said Q. "I'm not worth it."

Suddenly we heard the *beep-beep* of a car horn. We turned and saw Department Store Dad pulling up in front of the house. Beanpole jumped out of the vehicle, slammed the car door, and started running up to the front door. She was so excited she was practically popping out of her shoes.

Unfortunately, she was also so excited she didn't see the garden hose, tripped over a green loop of rubber, and did a gigantic face plop into a small mound of flowers.

"Ouch!"

She popped back up with daisy dirt in her hair.

"Don't worry, don't worry. I'm okay, I'm okay," she said as she wiped soil off her chin. "Hey, everyone, ready to go smash some ThreePees into chocolate pudding?"

There was a pause.

"I am!" I answered in an oh-so-perky way.

Q didn't respond.

"Hey, why aren't you dressed?" asked Beanpole when she saw Q.

Neither Q nor I responded. Beanpole paused, looked us over, then wrinkled her nose.

"What's going on?"

"Well, we had some small technical difficulties with Poochy," I answered. "But don't worry, he'll be okay."

"He's not going to be okay," Q said.

"What do you mean, *technical difficulties*? What's the problem?" asked Beanpole.

"I'm the problem," said Q. "I'm cursed. Anything I touch dies."

Q started walking away. "You guys should just go," she said. "Leave me alone. You're better off without me. The whole world is better off without me."

Q stalked down the hall. Beanpole and I stood in the doorway, unsure of what to do.

"What is she talking about?" Beanpole asked me. "I've never seen Q so depressed."

"Yesterday, after you left, the ThreePees stole Poochy from her and threw him into the Fountain while she was having one of her panic attacks," I said.

"Into the Fountain!" she exclaimed.

"But it's okay," I quickly added. "Marty is fixing him, and it's going to be okay."

"It is?" said Beanpole, unsure of how that could really be possible.

"Yes, it is," I said. Then I turned and yelled to Q, "Will you please get dressed? The show is gonna start and we need to get rolling."

Though Alice might have been feeling sad or pitiful or whatever, I knew that what she really needed was strength. Encouragement. "Positivity," as my mom would say. And though I don't know where it came from—I mean, I never really had an ounce of it in my life—suddenly I felt as if I were oozing with uplifting energy.

"Come on, let's go, girl," I shouted. "It's time to get dressed!"

Right then I felt like I had just one purpose in this whole entire world: get Q to the talent show. I just felt that if I could get her to the performing arts center, things were going to work out.

Somehow they would work out.

No, I didn't know how, but I knew they just had to. I mean, if you want to have rainbows, you gotta have rain, right? Well, in my opinion, our dorkasaurus mafia had had about enough rain to water an entire desert.

But there was something else, too. Something I was scared to even think about. For some reason I sensed that if I couldn't get Q to the talent show, I might not ever see her again.

Maybe no one would.

I gulped and tried not to think about that. After all, Q was about as sad as I had ever seen a thirteen-year-old girl in my life, and a person could only take so much, right?

I looked at the picture on the mantel of Q and her father wearing Mickey Mouse ears.

"Q!" I said, "I am telling you for the last time, go take off those ugly-butt pajamas and get dressed! We have to go."

Suddenly, we heard a voice from down the hall.

"Oh, hello there; you must be Barbara."

We all turned. It was Mrs. Applebee. She approached us, looking through her purse.

"Hi, nice to meet you," said Beanpole, greeting Q's mom with a smile and a handshake. "You have a very lovely home."

"Well, thank you," said Mrs. Applebee, impressed with Beanpole's good manners. I had to hand it to them: though the

Department Store Parents might have been weirdos, they certainly had raised Beanpole to be very polite.

"And this is Maureen," said Q in a low voice introducing me to her mother.

"Oh," answered Mrs. Applebee, "we already met."

Q raised her eyes, surprised by the news.

"You already met?"

Ssshh, ssshh, no, I thought.

"Yes," explained Mrs. Applebee. "Earlier. When Maureen came over."

"You came over?" asked Q in an almost accusatory manner.

"Yes, dear, when you were napping," explained Mrs. Applebee.

Ssshh, ssshh, no, I thought.

"Now, where is that..." Mrs. Applebee continued looking through her purse.

Q stared at me. "Why?" She started turning from sad to angry right in front of my eyes.

Gulp.

"Why?" I asked.

"Yes," said Q, crossing her arms. "Why?"

"To uh..." I started. "To, uh..." *Quick, Maureen, think. Think!* "To, uh...to tell you the good news. The good news that Marty was going to be able to fix Poochy!"

Phew! I thought. Close one.

Q stared at me with a deep, penetrating glare. She wasn't buying it.

"Now, come on," I said. "Get dressed. We've got a show to do."

"Oh, my lipstick," said Mrs. Applebee, mostly to herself. She closed her purse. "That's what I'm forgetting. Be right back."

She disappeared into the back bedroom.

Q stared at me with ever increasing anger. *Wheeesh-whooosh. Wheeesh-whooosh.*

"What?" I finally said.

"You're lying," Q answered. "I don't believe you."

"Lying about what?" I said.

"Lying about something, and I don't believe you. I don't believe"—*Wheeesh-whooosh. Wheeesh-whooosh*—"any of it."

"It's true," I said, trying to be as sincere as I could be, even though I was completely lying. "See, Marty did a . . . he did a . . ." *Quick Maureen, think!* "Marty did a backup."

"A backup?"

"I mean he made a backup," I said. *Come on, Maureen.* I started talking about a mile a minute. "You know how computer geeks are, they back up everything. That's how he was able to fix Poochy. See, he had a computer backup of all the brain stuff, and the rest of it was just wires and things, but you know how wires are wrapped in all that wirey stuff? Well, turns out Poochy wasn't under the water too long, and with the wires wrapped in the wirey stuff, and Marty having a backup of the computer brain, he fixed it, or rather, well, he is fixing it, so go get dressed."

Q stared. Beanpole stared too, her pink sweater sparkling. Right then I realized that if Beanpole didn't believe me, there was no way in the world that Q was going to believe me, either.

I waited for a response.

Wheeesh-whooosh. Wheeesh-whooosh.

It was quiet for about a hundred years. Q glared at me so intensely I couldn't even look up.

"Well," began Beanpole, "I guess if Marty said he could fix it..."

"He did!" I exclaimed. "I mean, by now he's almost done. And he's going to deliver it to the theater, and how lame would that be to let the ThreePees beat us because we didn't even show up? I mean, we have to show up. We just have to."

I waited for Q to respond.

"So..." I said. "What's it gonna be?"

There was another ten-hour pause.

Wheeesh-whooosh. Wheeesh-whooosh.

"Oh, come on, like let's go smash some ThreePees, huh?" I said in the perkiest voice I could muster. "Smash 'em like packages of chocolate-chip pudding."

"Chocolate-chip pudding?" said Beanpole.

"Did I say chocolate chip?" I said. "I meant..."

I turned to Q, my eyes begging her to trust me. To believe in me. To have faith in me.

Slowly, she took a step toward her bedroom door.

"Gimme a minute," she answered. "While I go get changed."

"To the Nerd Mobile!" said Q's mom.

Mrs. Applebee looked about as happy as I had ever seen an adult. Unfortunately, the three of us—Beanpole, Q, and I—were about as joyful as a rained-out holiday parade.

We got in the car, closed the doors, and fastened our seat belts.

"Oh, where's the fun, Nerd Girls?" asked Mrs. Applebee as she began driving. "A little nervous, huh?"

No one answered.

"Well, that's understandable," she offered. "But you're going to do fine this evening," she said. "I just know it, because when you hit that stage you'll have the one thing you need most."

She took a left at the traffic light.

"Each other," she said. "You'll have each other."

Beanpole and I were as silent as a piece of wood. Q took

a long, slow slurp off her scuba tank—*Wheeesh-whooosh. Wheeesh-whooosh*—and the car continued along.

Occasionally I looked over at Q. And occasionally she looked at me. But we never looked at each other at the same time. Either her eyes were staring out the window, or mine were staring out the window, but we both seemed to know to follow this rule: not to ever look at each other at the same time. Though we were in the same car going to the same place at the same time, Q and I might as well have been a bazillion miles apart.

A few minutes later we pulled into the parking lot and saw, like, ten thousand cars with all sorts of families getting ready to come see the talent show. When I recognized how far we'd have to park from the auditorium due to the lot being so full, the realization of just how many people were going to be in the audience that night hit me.

A lot. It would be a heck of a lot. I looked to the heavens.

Come on, Marty, you gotta come through. You just gotta.

Mrs. Applebee kissed Q on her forehead, wished us good luck, and left us to get a good seat for herself inside the auditorium. Beanpole, Q, and I, dressed in our outfits, walked around to the side of the building and then signed in backstage with Mr. Piddles.

"Nerd Girls, check," he said when he saw us. "Please wait in the assigned area. And good luck tonight." He smiled softly. "But based on what we saw yesterday, I'm not sure how much luck is going to play a part in this evening's show, right, girls?"

The three of us faked small smiles back at him, and then did as we were told, taking our proper places backstage while the audience took their seats. There was no sign of Marty anywhere.

Beanpole bit her fingernails. I looked at Q.

Wheeesh-whooosh. Wheeesh-whooosh.

We sat on our stools in silence. To our left, Disgusting Danny Dortenfuller loosened up his fingers for the cello. Turns out he was going to be able to perform, but with his booger-picking fingers still wrapped in all kinds of thick bandages from having been smashed by his father, no one expected him to be able to do much at all.

Wheeesh-whooosh. Wheeesh-whooosh.

We waited some more.

About ten minutes later the lights dimmed and Mr. Piddles took the stage and prepared to give a few welcoming announcements.

"Where's Marty?" Beanpole asked.

"Sshh," I said. "I want to hear this."

"Maureen," she asked again. "Where is Marty?"

"Don't worry, Beanpole," I said. "He'll be here. Now, I want to hear this."

Beanpole stared at me, then turned to Q to see what her thoughts on this matter were. Alice didn't say a word. Instead she just sat there dressed in her pretty, pink, sparkly little outfit, waiting for the nightmare of this entire evening to end.

Wheeesh-whooosh. Wheeesh-whooosh.

Come on, Marty, I thought. Come on.

Mr. Piddles took the microphone and made a joke about how all of the contestants were really talented, ending with the line,

"Even if their abilities might be less obvious to the untrained eye." The parents laughed. I think it was the same corny line he'd used for the past seventeen years, but still, the whole audience knew that what he was really explaining to them was that "Look, some of these kids absolutely stink, but please be nice and applaud and realize that they are trying their best tonight."

"Ha-ha!" I said with a big laugh in response to Mr. Piddles's joke. I turned to Beanpole and Q, trying to lighten the mood. "Mr. Piddles is a good teacher."

They stared at me like I was from another planet.

"Oh, just relax," I told them. "I'm sure Marty's gonna bring the dog in, like, five minutes, so be ready to rock it tonight, okay?"

Again, Beanpole bit her fingernails while Q looked at me with an unmistakable expression on her face: she had absolutely no desire to "rock it" at all.

Just then the ThreePees came out of their own private dressing room—of course—and took their positions on the other side of the backstage area, directly across from us. Thank goodness we couldn't hear them. But we could see them, all right. They were dressed in black and gold with peacock-style tails coming out of their butts. Top to bottom they shimmered like volts of high wattage, golden electricity.

The three of us stared. There was no doubt that with their hot bods, skintight outfits, and professional makeup, they looked absolutely great.

Just great.

Kiki puckered her lips and blew me a mean-spirited kiss. I lowered my eyes and looked away.

"Like, five minutes?" Beanpole asked in a hopeful manner after she saw Kiki taunt me.

"Like, five minutes," I answered. "For sure."

Ω just stared into the distance.

Wheeesh-whooosh. Wheeesh-whooosh.

Come on, Marty, I prayed. *Please, you gotta come through.*

alentless loser after talentless loser hit the stage, but all the parents were nice and proud and understanding, and after each act, they politely applauded.

"You know, if Spacey Susie learned not to drop her clarinet, she might become a real force in the music scene one day," I said, referring to Susie Clayborne as she exited the stage.

Q stared at me. I lowered my eyes and avoided her gaze.

"Where the heck is Poochy?" demanded Beanpole. "You said five minutes and it's been like seventy-five!"

"Oh look," I said, turning my attention back to the show. "Max is gonna jump on the pogo stick. I love pogo sticks. Don't you guys love pogo sticks?"

"Maureen!" shouted Beanpole, grabbing me by the shoulder and spinning me around. "Where is Poochy?"

I stared at her with a frightened look.

"I told you, Marty's going to bring it," I said uncertainly.

"He's not gonna bring it," said Q. "He's not gonna bring it at all."

Q stood up.

"He is," I said, "Look!"

And just then, like some sort of Christmas miracle, Marty showed up backstage carrying a black bag.

"See, I told you." I said.

I rushed up to Marty and lunged for the bag.

"Finally," I said to him. "I mean, goodness gracious."

I looked up. Marty was low-key and quiet.

"What?" I said. I could see there was something he wanted to say. "What? Spill it," I repeated.

"Sorry," he said. "I tried."

I reached inside the bag and pulled out Poochy. I paused. The dog, well, it looked okay. I mean, at least its head was attached.

I turned on the power. Nothing. I flipped the switch a second time . . . and then a third.

Still nothing. Nothing at all. Poochy was still dead.

"Like I said," Marty said, "sorry."

"And now, for our next performance," announced Mr. Piddles. "It's going to Rain Gold!"

Boom! An explosion blasted through the theater and the lights went pitch black. A moment later, gold confetti dropped from the rafters, and a few seconds after that a burst of rainbow lights hit center stage.

Then, as if by magic, the ThreePees appeared through a cloud of smoke. It was an awe-inspiring entrance.

"But those little witches," Marty commented under his breath, "they're gonna pay."

He walked away.

The three of us stared at the stage. A hard beat pumped, and the music began. Some kind of cinematic journey through the plains of Africa played on the fifty-foot projection screen behind the ThreePees. The audience was electrified.

We watched for a minute, silent and unmoving. Finally, I spoke.

"Well, we can still do it," I said, optimistically, as I grabbed Poochy's leash. Beanpole and Q stared at me. "I mean, we can still do some kind of makeshift performance. You know, where we drag him around by his leash and he dances in sync with us while we..."

Holding the leash, I began to march like we were doing our routine, in order to show them how we could still get the dog to kinda follow along if we stayed with the original plan.

But then Poochy's head fell off.

I stopped. The robotic dog was totally and completely destroyed. Beanpole and Q stared at me, wondering what I would do next.

"Okay, okay, don't worry," I said as I came up with Plan B. "We can still—"

"She told you, didn't she?"

"What?" I said. "Told me what? I have no idea what you're talking about, but look, we can still—"

"She told you," said Q with a shake of her head, as I fumbled with the broken dog. "I knew it. She told you."

"Told her what?" asked Beanpole.

I didn't respond. The ThreePees danced in the background.

"Would somebody please tell me what is going on?" Bean-pole demanded.

I stood and walked up to Alice.

"You look nice tonight," I said. "I mean, that outfit, well... it kinda flatters you."

"What?!" exclaimed Beanpole. "Did you just say she looks nice?"

It appeared that Beanpole's ears were going to pop off, she was so angry.

"You pick right now to say the first nice thing you've ever said to any of us? Right now, Maureen?" she shouted.

"What I meant was that your mom, Beanpole, she did a really nice job of covering Q's—"

"I knew she told you," exclaimed Q, pushing me away. "I knew it!"

She collapsed into a chair.

"She had no right!" she yelled out. "She had no right!"

She began to cry. I turned and looked out at the ThreePees. Sofes O'Reilly approached the big turn.

And nailed it. She hit it perfectly.

Then, like NFL cheerleaders, the ThreePees sprang into the air, jumped over a ring of fire, and landed in a synchronized split that would have been good enough to win a gold medal at the Olympics.

"Aren't I pathetic enough without her?" said Q. "Aren't I a big enough loser without her interference? Why does she always think she has to protect me?"

"It's not like that, Alice," I said. "It's not like that at all."

"Would somebody please tell me what's going on?" said Beanpole.

Suddenly, there was a blast of explosions. Indoor fireworks, the color of gold. The crowd went nuts.

"G'head, tell her," said Q.

I didn't answer.

"G'head," said Q, her eyes blazing with rage. "Tell her what a monster I am. Tell her what a bad person I am. Tell her about how I am a selfish little spoiled brat who killed her family because she wanted to play a stupid video game. Tell her. Tell her!"

I didn't move.

"Tell her!" Q shouted. Her eyes were red with tears and rage. "Tell her how I deserve to die!!!"

I stood there stunned.

"TELL HER!!!" screamed Alice.

"And now, for our final performance..." said Mr. Piddles as the ThreePees bounced off the stage. "Please put your hands together for the Nerd Girls."

We heard a small round of applause. None of us moved.

"Um, Nerd Girls?" repeated Mr. Piddles into the microphone. "Nerd Girls, it's your turn."

We could hear the people shuffling in their seats while the stage sat empty. A long fifteen seconds passed, nobody knowing what to do or how to respond.

"Um, Nerd Girls?" said Mr. Piddles again. "Last call."

"You're not a monster, Alice," I said. "And you're not a bad person, either."

I lifted my head and looked her in the eyes.

"And you don't deserve to die."

"Oh yeah?" she barked at me. "Then what am I? What am I, Maureen? Tell me!"

I paused.

"You're just sad, Alice. On the inside, you're just sad, and you need to let it out."

I lowered my eyes and began walking toward the stage.

"Wait!" said Beanpole. "Where are you going?"

"Out there," I answered.

"What?" exclaimed Beanpole.

"I am going out there," I repeated.

"But why?" she asked.

"I don't know," I answered. "I guess because I just realized that none of this is about a dog."

My words hung in the air.

"And if we don't go out there, they win."

I turned, took a deep breath, and walked out to center stage.

The spotlight hit me in the face. Hundreds of people stared.

Actually, a thousand.

I picked up the microphone. It took me a moment to begin.

"I..." *BEERREERRRRERPPPPP!!!*

A burst of feedback pierced everybody's ears. I guess I'd put the mike too close to my mouth or something.

"Sorry," I said. The audience didn't seem too happy.

Everyone stared and waited. It took a moment before I started again.

"Um, I'm not sure I have any talent," I said into the mike.

The audience shifted uncomfortably in their seats.

"I'm not even sure I—"

Suddenly I was interrupted by an image on the projection screen. It whirled to life behind me.

Huh?

I looked up, and a video started playing.

It was the YouTube video of A Chunky Chick Does the Peanut-Butter-and-Mango-Marmalade Big Butt Dance. It only took a few seconds before the audience began to laugh and howl.

I turned and looked over at the ThreePees. They were high-fiving each other backstage.

I looked back at the big screen and watched as I squished peanut-butter-and-mango-marmalade sandwiches into my face and went "*Mrrmphh Mrrmphh Mrrmphh*" in front of a thousand people.

"You know," I finally said into the mike as the video continued to play behind me, "that was once the worst moment of my life."

"I can see why!" someone yelled. The comment got a big laugh.

"Yeah, the worst," I admitted. "But now, well . . . now, I actually think it's kind of small potatoes."

The audience got quiet. I looked out into the crowd. It was hard to see any faces with all the lights shining in my eyes, but I could tell they were listening.

"Yeah, small potatoes, because, see, I did that for my friend." I pointed to the screen, and everyone watched as I ran around like a stupid, fat, sweaty pig with a face stuffed full of food.

"My friend Alice."

I turned to look backstage at Q. I started to cry.

I saw Beanpole walk over to Alice to ask her what was going on. Then I saw Q turn and whisper something in Beanpole's ear. Though I couldn't hear their conversation, I was pretty sure I knew what Q was telling her.

At first Beanpole looked shocked. Then I saw her lean over and hug Q.

"That's right," I loudly announced into the mike as I turned to face the audience. "I am friends with Allergy Alice Applebee." A rush of energy came over me. "And I know something about her," I continued. "Something about her that almost no one else in this theater knows."

I smiled big and proud.

"And you know what?" I said. "I think I have something to tell you about this little secret of hers. Something to tell all of you!"

I turned and saw the expression on Q's face suddenly change to freak-out level, full of fear and anxiety and horror.

"Yep, I sure do," I said. "I sure do. And here it is…"

I paused, making sure to speak loudly and clearly so that everyone in the entire auditorium would be able to hear me.

"I will never say a word, you hear me? I'm not saying a word. Never! " I told the crowd. "Because real friends, that's what they do. They keep each other's secrets and they have each other's backs and they're there for each other when times get tough."

I looked at Q. She seemed completely shocked by my words, as if she had no idea how to respond.

"You hear me?!" I repeated into the microphone. "I am

friends with weirdo, freak-a-zoid Allergy Alice Applebee, the turdball, doof-brain, kook-job of the century, and I don't care who knows it. I'm proud of it! I am proud that she is my friend!"

I turned again and looked at Q. Tears streamed from my eyes. Suddenly, Alice began walking toward me, toward center stage.

She took the mike.

"And I am friends with Maureen—the baked potato, peanut-butter-squishing-cupcake-lover—Saunders," she said. "Best friends."

We hugged and cried.

"Did you just call me a baked potato in front of a thousand people?" I asked as tears poured down my face.

"Uh-huh," she said with a laugh.

I paused.

"You're funny," I told her.

"And you're weird," she replied.

"But I'm not trying to be weird," I said.

"And I'm not trying to be funny," she answered.

We laughed and hugged again, the tears just flowing and flowing and flowing. A moment later, we turned to Beanpole, who was standing all by herself backstage, and waved at her to come out and join us.

A huge smile crossed her face, and she started to run as fast as she could.

But of course she tripped over the microphone cord.

"OUCH!" she yelped as she did a face-plant center stage.

"OOOHHH," gasped the audience. Beanpole looked as if she had just killed herself. But then she bounced up off the hardwood floor and took the mike.

"I'm okay, I'm okay. Don't worry," she said. "I'm okay."

The three of us hugged and laughed and smiled and cried. The people in the audience had no idea what was going on. Absolutely none. A moment later, we heard a voice over the loudspeaker.

"Um, Nerd Girls," asked Mr. Piddles from his judge's chair, "do we have a talent to perform?"

We looked out into the crowd. The audience stared in amazement, waiting to see what we were going to do next. I grabbed the mike.

"Do we have a talent?" I said in a sarcastic tone. "Of course we have a talent," I answered.

I took a step back.

"Hit 'em, Beanpole."

Barbara paused, unsure of what I meant. But then, a moment later, she understood what I was talking about and reached into her sock.

Where she pulled out a Q-tip.

A moment later, off came her shoe.

Alice and I stepped back as Beanpole proceeded to clean the wax out of her ear using only her big toe to hold the cotton swab. In a middle-school talent show filled with loser performances, it was by far the biggest loser performance of all.

Q and I just smiled as Barbara worked furiously to impress the crowd. I could even hear a small *squeak, squeak* coming from her left ear. Wanting to help Beanpole out as best I could, I got down on my hands and knees and stuck out my own head, and Beanpole moved from cleaning her ears with a Q-tip to cleaning mine.

The audience gasped. Beanpole didn't even flip the cotton swab around: it just went straight from her ear to mine.

"*Urrggh,*" groaned the crowd. I smiled.

A moment later Alice bent down, and before anyone realized it, Beanpole was cleaning all of our ears with the same Q-tip. To tell the truth, she was pretty good.

Finally, with the audience staring at us like we were the biggest freaks they had ever witnessed, we stood up, grabbed the mike, and shouted "NERD GIRLS!" before we dashed off the stage.

When we got backstage, behind the curtain, we were all silly with the giggles. The ThreePees stormed up.

"What kind of dorkfest was that?" asked Kiki, apparently outraged that we were having a good time.

"Like, did you just share the same Q-tip?" asked Brattany.

"Gross!" said Sofes. "That's like, so not hypodermic."

"Hygienic, Sofes," said Kiki. "The word is hygienic."

"Uh, yeah...whatever."

"And now"—Mr. Piddles's voice came over the loudspeaker— "if we could please have all the contestants return to the stage."

The house lights in the theater went on, and the audience moved to the edge of their seats. Every kid who had performed walked to the center of the stage. Beanpole, Q, and I had our arms interlocked together super tight. There was nothing that could break apart our grip on one another. Nothing at all.

"While everyone who appeared this evening is a winner," announced Mr. Piddles, "there can only be one performance that is awarded the Grover Middle School Grand Prize for Aptitude. And so, without further ado..."

He paused for dramatic effect.

"Drumroll, please..." He stalled as if he were creating even more drama.

"RAIN OF GOLD!" he shouted as the music started. Suddenly, more confetti and balloons dropped from the rafters, and the audience let out a huge cheer.

The ThreePees ran to the front of the stage and started hugging and kissing one another like a group of Miss Americas.

The audience stood on its feet and clapped loudly.

"Picture! Picture!" someone called out. "The yearbook picture!"

Just then each of the girls was handed a bouquet of roses. Kiki and Brittany-Brattany and Sofes took a step back and smiled for the camera.

"Wait," came a voice. It was Marty. "The stage lights, they're making your foreheads look too shiny," he told them. "Quick, pat yourselves down with this makeup. We want to get a good shot."

The ThreePees started patting down their faces with makeup pads, just like the Hollywood celebrities do to make sure that their foreheads aren't too shiny under the bright lights.

"Make sure you do your eyebrows," Marty said. "Do 'em good." I guess since Marty was wearing a tie, they trusted him.

But they shouldn't have. That's because Marty had put hair remover in the makeup kit.

"There...perfect...Okay, smile girls!" said Marty taking a step backward.

Poof! Flashbulbs went off.

A minute later Kiki's mother and sisters ran up onstage to give Kiki a big hug and congratulations.

Then they froze.

"Oh my goodness, what happened?" asked Kiki's mom.

"We won!" shouted Kiki, holding the bouquet of roses. "Mommy, we won!"

"No, I mean to your eyebrows," said Kiki's mother. "Where are your eyebrows?"

"What?" said Kiki, the smile vanishing from her face. She turned to look at Brittany-Brattany, then Sofes.

Their eyebrows were gone too.

"Oh my gawd, you look like chicken eggs!"

"Smile, girls!" said Marty with a huge grin on his face, holding a video camera. "Smile big for YouTube!"

Having no idea what was happening, the ThreePees stood there like a group of stupefied, eyebrow-less girls who had just traveled to Earth from Planet Alien Egg. A moment later, a look of fear and shock swept over their faces, and they tried to run. However, with all the people onstage, the ThreePees hadn't noticed that Ashley and her group of gymnastic friends had formed a circle around them so that there was no way for the ThreePees to escape.

They were trapped.

"Snobby Witches with No Eyebrows Win the Talent Show ...Smile girls! This could break the one million hit mark on YouTube!"

The ThreePees fought to escape the circle, but Ashley and her gymnast friends were really strong for young kids, and neither Kiki, Brittany-Brattany, nor Sofes could get away.

Kiki's mom and sisters tried to help, but all the Masters

family was able to do was cause more chaos and add more funny footage to the video.

Especially when Miss Masters's wig fell off.

"Mommy, help me!"

"Let go, you brat!"

Ashley stomped the foot of Cece Masters.

"Ow, you dwarf!"

Suddenly there was a countdown...

"Three...two...one!"

The gymnast girls let go, and everyone onstage took off running.

For the Fountain, where we all jumped in.

"This was the best talent show ever," I said, splashing Q.

"I'm allergic to chlorine," she shouted back with the biggest smile on her face that I had ever seen. Then she splashed Beanpole and dunked herself completely under the water. Marty, video camera in hand, filmed everything, especially Q's smile.

"Who are we? Who are we? Who are we?" I shouted, my pink sparkly costume soaking wet top to bottom.

Beanpole, Q, and I looked at one another, then screamed as loud as we could.

"NERD GIRLS!!!"

Oh, was there chaos the next Monday at school. Kiki's mom, along with all the kids who were involved in the fiasco—plus all of their parents—were in the principal's office by seven thirty a.m., and the heat was turned up to full blast. Kiki's mom demanded expulsion, jail time, and, most important of all, a retake of the yearbook picture.

"But it will have to wait because it will be at least four months before the girls' eyebrows grow back," she said.

Mr. Piddles was there as well. He studied me with curious eyes.

"Might I ask what happened to the robotic-dog dance routine?" he said.

The room got quiet, and everyone turned to me. My mom, Q and her mom, Beanpole and her parents, all of the ThreePees and their parents, everyone, they just looked at me.

I turned and stared at Kiki and her pet donkeys. Their

expressions changed from innocent little victims of a terrible crime to mean and nasty perpetrators of a crime of their own.

I paused. *Wow, did their* no-eyebrow faces make them look super weirdo.

"Do you want the truth?" I said to Mr. Piddles.

"Of course," he answered.

The principal, Mr. Mazer, waited. He was a firm man who didn't like any monkey business. My mom put her hand on my back to show that she was with me one hundred percent.

"Well," I began. The ThreePees lowered their eyes. They knew they were toast. "We decided to go in a different direction."

"A different direction?" asked Mr. Piddles. I could tell he didn't believe me. The ThreePees looked up at the same time with surprised, eyebrowless expressions. Their faces really did look like chicken eggs.

"Yep," I said. "A different direction."

"You mean you chose to give an almost incomprehensible speech and then share a cotton swab in all of your ears, as opposed to doing an elaborate dance routine with a robotic dog, which had obviously taken a great many hours to prepare?" said Mr. Piddles.

"Uh-huh," I said. "That's right. We decided to go with the Q-tip."

"But why would you make such a decision?" asked Mr. Piddles. He was determined to get to the bottom of this.

"Because, we're Nerd Girls," I answered. "And that's just how Nerd Girls roll."

Beanpole came over and put her hand in mine. Q came over and grabbed my other hand. The whole room stared at us.

The message was clear: *Do what you will to us; we aren't budging.*

After a moment, Mr. Mazer rose from his chair. All the adults stared. The parents of the ThreePees wanted answers, and the tension in the room got even thicker. Not a sound could be heard.

Not a sound except one...

Wheeesh-whooosh. Wheeesh-whooosh.

"You're such a dorkasaurus," I said to Q.

"Look who's talking," she answered with a smile.

"Hey," said Beanpole, not wanting to be left out. "I'm a dorkasaurus too."

"Oh yes you are, Beanpole. Yes you are," I said.

She smiled, happy to be properly insulted.

"Um, ladies, if you don't mind," said Principal Mazer, "I have other things to do in this lifetime. Now, Mr. Piddles, if you please..." He nodded his head.

Mr. Piddles opened up his laptop computer and showed the yearbook picture to everyone in the room. The eyebrowless Miss America photo was the funniest picture I'd ever seen.

"You know, this photograph, if I may interrupt," said Mr. Piddles, addressing the room. "For some reason, it strikes me as ...what's the word I am looking for?"

"Abominable?" said Kiki's mother. "Horrible? Freakish?" she added.

"No, that's not it," answered Mr. Piddles. "This picture, for some reason, it strikes me as...*just.* Yes, that's the word I am looking for. *Just.*"

"Listen to me; you can't put that picture in the yearbook!" exclaimed Brittany-Brattany's dad. "I'll sue!"

"Yeah," said the father of Sofes. "We'll sue."

"Oh, I wasn't going to publish the picture," answered Mr. Piddles calmly. "Consider it deleted."

Mr. Piddles pushed the delete button on his computer, and the shot of the ThreePees vanished forever.

Too bad, I thought.

"And I demand you take that video off of YouTube as well," added Kiki's mother. "I've never been so mortified."

"Miss Masters," said Mr. Piddles, "if I had the power to take a video off of YouTube, do you really think I'd still be a middle-school social studies teacher?"

The parents of the ThreePees turned to Mr. Mazer. He shrugged. "What, you think I'd be a middle-school principal?" he asked. "Sorry, we can't help you there."

"But the entire world can see it," Kiki's mother pleaded. "It's already had eleven thousand hits."

"Sixteen thousand, seven hundred and twenty-five hits as of 7:03 this morning," said Q.

Everyone turned to look at Alice.

"Accurate statistics are important to her," I said, clearing up the matter.

"You haven't heard the end of this," said Kiki's mom as she stormed out of the office. "I want justice. I mean, look at my child, she's a monster!"

"She was a monster before she lost her eyebrows," Beanpole said.

"Barbara," snapped Department Store Mom. "That wasn't nice. That wasn't nice at all."

"Sorry, Mom," said Beanpole. "But you know what? Sometimes in this world you can't always be nice. Some people"—she stared at the ThreePees—"some people need to be treated a little differently."

Beanpole glared at the ThreePees. They glared back. Q and I got right next to Beanpole, and suddenly we found ourselves in a huge staring match once again.

"You little nerd brats haven't heard the end of this," Kiki's mom threatened as she stormed out of the office. "You haven't heard the end of this at all."

With that, Kiki and her mother bolted out of the room. The donkeys and their parents followed right behind her.

"Now, listen to me, young ladies, and listen to me good," said Principal Mazer in a firm tone. "I want this over with. You got me, Nerd Girls? I'm serious. I don't want to see any more problems between you and those girls. Am I clear?"

Q raised the scuba tank to her lips, then stared off into the distance like a Wild West gunfighter. Through the principal's window, we could see that the ThreePees had gathered by the front of the Fountain. It was obvious that they were already scheming a way to get back at us.

"I don't think you'll be having more trouble with us, Mr. Principal, but"—*Wheeesh-whooosh. Wheeesh-whooosh*—"something tells me, us Nerd Girls ain't seen the last of them."

The principal turned and looked out the window.

Q squinted and stared into the distance.

"Nope"—*Wheeesh-whooosh. Wheeesh-whooosh*—"we ain't seen the last of them."

We walked outside and said good-bye to our parents. Once all the adults had left, we got ready to go to our separate classes.

"See you guys at lunch?" Q asked.

"Can't wait," I answered. "Hey, Beanpole, what'd your mom make you today, anyway?"

"Lasagna," she answered. "Shaped like a boxing glove."

"Like a boxing glove?" I said.

"Yeah," Beanpole replied. " 'Cause even though my mommy wants me to be nice, she also wants me to stand up for myself."

Q stared across the courtyard. The ThreePees glared back at us.

"Hey, Maureen, Maureen," a voice suddenly called out from behind me. I turned around.

It was Logan Meyers.

"Would it be like, stupid, if I, like, wanted to carry your books for you?" He stared all googly-eyed at me like a lost puppy.

"Nah, thanks though, Logan," I answered. "I got it."

"Well, maybe tomorrow?" he asked in a hopeful voice.

"Mm," I said. "I don't think so."

"Well," he answered, backing away, "like maybe you'll change your mind, right? You gotta think positive, right, Maureen? Right?"

"Ya know, Logan, thinking positive's not stupid," I told him. "At least not stupid like stupid video games," I added.

He paused and wrinkled his forehead.

"Um, yeah…I know exactly what you mean," he answered,

even though I could tell he had no idea what I was talking about. "I know exactly what you mean."

I smiled.

"Well, see ya later, maybe!" he called out, and then dashed off to go to his first-period class. I looked up at Beanpole and Q.

"I just wish I could get that kid off my jock."

We broke out in a big laugh.

"See ya."

"See ya."

"See you guys later," I said as I walked away, and for the first time that I could ever remember, I was really, really, really looking forward to lunch.

After all, what could be more fun than hanging out with a couple of Nerd Girls?